ac

AFTER YOU

AFTER YOU

A Novel

by Annie Garrett

St. Martin's Press

New York

Design by Songhee Kim

ISBN 0-312-19671-7

For Jeremiah Garrett,
without whom...

Nobody had told her that years pivoted on nothing but moments. Nobody had warned that disasters, like miracles, were the work of mere impulse but lasted forever. Nobody had urged her to be careful of the details because they were linked and fragile as the daisy chains she had made that summer in Maine when the sky blurred blue against the deep hue of the ocean and when the breeze was cool and the sun was warm. Nobody had told her that every life, that her life too, was a daisy chain. But, driving north, she could see at last that it was. She had learned that lesson on her own these past weeks, had earned that grave, yet beautiful, truth.

A few links of the daisy chain: Her father had always admired the *heft of Burl Ives's voice and had often played folk music on the living room hi-fi. His favorite song was "Down in the Valley," and when Clare was a baby, he had sung it to her as a lullaby. Years later, after she was grown and had moved away and married, her father sprained his knee in a pothole while jogging. He confessed his injury to Clare long-distance that Saturday morning during his weekly phone visit, and of course she fretted the rest of the day and berated herself for not living closer to him. That evening, Clare had heard Garrison Keillor singing "Down in the Valley" on the radio. And because she was worried about her dad and wanted him to know, she tried to make a tape of her old lullaby. But because she was a klutz with anything that plugged in and had buttons, she botched the attempt.*

Then, still years later, a few more daisies: Today, hurrying out of the house for maybe the last time, she had dropped some cassette tapes and had tossed them all back into their box so haphazardly that they spilled out and rattled on the backseat floorboard. As she swerved down the highway's on-ramp, the clattering they made reminded her that she didn't have to subject herself to Dr. Laura's advice on the radio, which was strident as a guilty conscience. Solace was within reach: music. So Clare had groped blindly behind her seat for a tape and had picked up this one.

And what she heard, as she pulled her Saturn into the fast lane heading north, was "Down in the Valley" on a poor-quality homemade recording. Clare could not recall the details of the night she had tried to capture the song off the radio, not specifically. She did remember the time in her life, could almost see the scene. It would have been early in her marriage to Michael, when they were living in Brooklyn. Those were the years when they stayed home on Saturday nights and made supper while listening to the radio show that was broadcast off the prairie where she had grown up. Earlier in the day, she and Michael would have slept late and then walked to the farmers' market up by the park, and later they would likely have been planning to watch a videotape, something in warm black and white with Ingrid Bergman or Cary Grant or both. *It was what they could afford for entertainment—NPR and three-dollar videos and their own cooking. But they hadn't felt pinched by it. Maybe there were fresh raspberries, and raindrops clattering on the window. Maybe the brownstone apartment was yellow with candlelight. Maybe later they would make love once, or three times.*

Remembering this, she started to eject the tape. She wasn't in the mood for sentimental. Down in the valley, the valley so low. Hang your head over, hear the wind blow. *She needed something lively and renegade, something that would let her mind spin beyond itself, away from any part of herself that might still question what she was doing on this crowded coastal highway, where she was going, to whom. She was riding on her impulse, her nerve, her anger. She wanted music that would help carry her along. She wanted something as stirring and jagged and primal as her own motivations.*

Her finger was on the eject button of the car stereo when she heard the other voices, the ones in the background, the ones that weren't supposed to be there. The first one she recognized, after a confused minute, as her own. She heard herself say loudly, "Damn, damn. Is that right? I can't figure this thing out."

Michael said, from farther off, "Did you get it?"

She answered, "I think so, technological twit that I am. Check it, though, would you?"

Beep. Beep. Beep. The timer on the oven bleated in the background.

"If you'll get the bread out," *Michael said.* "See if it sounds hollow, though—I didn't thump it yet." *His voice moved closer, grew bolder on the tape. Their footsteps sounded across the hardwoods, thudding in socks, changing places.* "Oh, Clarie," *he snorted affectionately, up close to the microphone now.* "What did you do to this?"

Her answer seemed to echo from far away, from the kitchen. She yelped. "Ow, ow, ow."

His voice faded as he got distracted from his task and went to help her. "What? Did you burn yourself? Let's see," *he said.*

Angels in heaven, know I love you. Know I love you, dear, know I love you.

⎯℃℃⎯

For a while, as Clare moved the Saturn in and out of the passing lane, driving fast, she could hear the murmuring of the two of them off in the kitchen, maybe a decade earlier. Garrison Keillor finished his song, and the show carried on with sound effects of chickens squawking and then an Irish soprano sang a love song for a river. But Clare, with both hands on the wheel now, was listening beyond that and hard, listening for what was happening in her old life, straining to eavesdrop on Michael fussing over her burned hand. She tried to hear into that night she had lived already in her life. And had forgotten.

When she hit the Connecticut stateline, the voices on the tape came closer. Michael said, "I forgot the wine."

"Got it," she said.

There was rustling, and in her memory Clare could see the two of them settling on the couch where they always ate, he at one end and she at the other, their legs bent, their stocking feet touching in the middle. She was sure they would have lifted their glasses to toast one another with Gallo's cheap French Colombard.

"The shallots are sweeter roasted this way," he said.

"They were a good idea," she agreed.

They ate in silence for a while. "More wine?" he asked.

"Sure."

As she drove and listened, Clare thought how those days, those years even, were nothing but a few snapshots in an old album now: Michael looking tired but elated standing among boxes the day they moved in together; Clare peeling a butternut squash the first Thanksgiving after they were married; the two of them holding hands, barefoot on the beach with their shadows blown behind them like scarves. Those years were nothing but yellowing photographs and these voices—his and hers—imprinted on metal tape by some magnetic process she couldn't comprehend but which was ephemeral, she knew, ephemeral as words on paper and light on negatives and vows on a human heart. Magnetism could ruin tapes, she had been taught, could ruin them as easily as it could create them. It could erase computer memory. It could blot out sound. "Keep that magnet away from your watch," Dad had warned when she was little, "or you're not going to have a watch at all." Magnetism could even stop time.

And time had stopped, hadn't it? That time in their lives anyway, in their marriage. It was lost to her, as Michael was. He merely sounded so close.

On the tape, he exhaled satisfaction loudly, and her old self answered him with a comfortable laugh.

"The bread is amazing," he said.

"You think the rosemary works in it?"

"Best you've ever made."

"You always say that," she admonished him.

"I mean it every time."

That was all. The tape pulled up short. The time ran out. As it always does. And even as Clare held her foot steady on the accelerator and her hand on the gearshift, even as her eyes searched the road ahead, she knew it was one of those moments, that her life was turning, that uncovering this accidental tape was another link, another seemingly insignificant detail, another terribly fragile daisy in the chain of her life.

Part One

It began with a postcard. But it was the timing of the card's arrival that mattered, that old crux. When Clare was single and working as a news assistant in the city, she and JoJo had sometimes consoled one another over failed romances by eating chocolate on a bench in Central Park and by telling each other that it was just the timing that was off for this one. Another time, *this* one would've worked. Clare hadn't really believed it though. Back then, she and JoJo were putting in twelve-hour days but were still making only enough money to share a third-floor walk-up where often they dragged in after midnight and ate cold sesame noodles off paper plates and then soaked themselves in succession in the clawfoot tub that stood on a platform in the middle of the kitchen. Their shoulders and necks ached. "Stress bruises," they called the pain, saying it came from the everyday exercise of stroking too many egos higher up.

Clare wanted desperately then to believe in the rescue of timing, that some day, some hour, some minute, the planets would line up or the sun would shine from just the right angle or the moon would hold her good fortune in the cup of its waxing or waning. But she had already seen enough to believe instead that she and JoJo were merely saying or doing or eating anything that would make them feel better. Once, when their brownie fell on the ground under a park bench, they had actually brushed off the ants and eaten it, mad for its chemical jolt of approximated love. So Clare had thought that blaming the timing was one of those hollow but supposedly palliative things that people did. It was like saying that someone who had just died of cancer was better off—"freed from suffering"— when actually the poor woman would have been better off never to have found that lump in her breast and never to have had the doctor confirm the worst and never to have sickened until her hair fell out and never to have planned her own funeral, complete with Iris Dement singing "My Life." A swift death was about as much compensation for a long happy life as a brownie was for love.

But years later, when Clare called JoJo and told her to cancel whatever professional lunch plans she had programmed into her pocket computer—on that afternoon when she met JoJo at the midtown sushi restaurant where the waiter automatically knew to bring them two Diet Cokes with lemon, low-sodium soy sauce, extra wasabi, extra ginger, and a fork for JoJo, when Clare finally told her oldest, dearest friend about the postcard—Clare admitted that the powerful thing about it, more than what it said or where it came from or who sent it, was *when* it had come: the timing.

"What, you had PMS?" JoJo had cracked.

"Worse," Clare had assured her. Much worse.

—⌒⌒—

The postcard had slipped from the mailman's fingers and had fallen through the brass mail slot into their little house, far upriver from the city. It landed on the hardwood floor that gleamed at the edges of the Persian rugs, landed as the ceiling fan thumped lazily but steadily, as the hollyhocks and delphiniums bloomed headily along the fence. It slid away from the catalogs that had been folded around it, away from the envelopes. It slid with the whisper of a swish and lodged under one leg of the old pharmacist's desk where Michael paid the bills. Just like other postcards on other days.

But on this day, Clare's eyes were puffed and sore from a night of crying. On this day, Michael was out of her reach, and her own inner resources had been spent by working five months straight, seven days a week, covering the trial of a movie star accused of molesting his wife's thirteen-year-old sister. Clare had been given time off to recover from the ordeal, which had taken her to the West Coast, where she had been expected to do live coverage for the network's late news show in L.A., as well as the early one in New York. She had lived on Starbucks and next to no sleep and on snatched phone calls to Michael. And, as it turned out, that had suited her fine. Now that it was over and she was home at last, she had too much time to think, and sometimes, when she was sunk in that thinking, she went and stood in front of the mirror and opened her blouse and made herself look, made herself listen to her worst thoughts. *Maybe still. But when?*

As the mail fell through the slot, she was standing in front of the mirror that way. Her stronger half was rebuking the weaker for not doing something healthy. For not weeding the tomato patch. For not deadheading the roses. For not taking a book out onto the porch and snuggling up in the rocking chair she and Michael had found for sale by the road in Vermont, the rocking chair where she had sworn she would someday sit and watch the Hudson go by and reread every Jane Austen novel and then every word of the fragments. If ever, now was a day to begin. *Sense and Sensibility* was on the shelf. The trial of the movie star was over. He was free. Her own personal trials were over now, by a year, and she too was free. Or so they told her, assured her. But she knew, measuring herself in the mirror, that she would never be free. Because she would never be sure.

"It was a pure pity party," was how she later explained it to JoJo as she tried to tweeze a sesame seed out of the soy sauce.

"You should've called me," JoJo said, through a mouthful of yellowtail. "You had my itinerary, didn't you?"

"My life is one *should've* after the other," Clare reminded her.

❧❧

The mailman's footfalls on the porch that day had startled Clare, and she had hurriedly buttoned her shirt, as though she'd been caught poking around in somebody else's lingerie drawer. Her first thought was to ignore the mail, let it lie. There would likely be a reminder from Dr. Bladoe's office about her upcoming appointment to undergo the battery of quarterly tests. She couldn't face that, and there was no one else she could stand to hear from just now. Even the prospect of a postcard from JoJo's African safari honeymoon offered no comfort. She was feeling that raw.

But by the next thought, she had decided maybe Michael had sent something. Maybe he might have found a way to squeeze in a note from the chaos of his parents' house, might have known she needed one of the little haikus that he sometimes scratched out on coffee-shop napkins and left on her pillow. Or maybe there would be a flower like the pansy he had pressed dry and sent to the hotel in L.A., alone in its envelope, no words necessary. And so she walked into the front room and reached for the pile of mail.

The postcard snagged her peripheral vision, and she bent again. It was from Maine. The picture on the front was of a lobster. Underneath, was printed one word: LOBSTUH. She grinned and said it out loud, suspecting that Michael might have found the card among his mother's things and had sent it as a joke, knowing so well what would make her smile.

The Maine accent was one of the things Clare had immediately loved when, at age seventeen, she had arrived for the one summer she spent Down East. She loved how open-sounding the accent was, as though the tongue were a screen door that swung on a tight hinge, in and out on each word. Of course, hers had been the odd accent, the foreign one on that coast. Her own inflections, or lack thereof, must have seemed flat as the Minnesota prairie to the locals she met. But theirs seemed so marvelous to her that she repeated whole phrases when she heard them, took them into her own mouth, swung them on her own tongue. People slipped looks at her from under their eyelashes, and it took her a while to discern that they were often insulted. They were so reserved she found it difficult to read them the way she could read the people back home, and when she finally figured out that they felt hurt by what she had thought was homage to their speech, she was appalled. She had been quoting them back to herself like Keats or Shakespeare, and they had thought she was cruelly parroting them. That was the summer she began to learn that she did not unerringly move through the world, that she did not always discern black from white. That lesson happened in little things and big.

She was in Maine to spend the summer with her aunt Fran and

uncle Tig. Her parents had sent her away, they said, to enjoy herself. But Clare knew that it was because her mother was dying. They didn't tell her that at the time, of course. They gave her the trip as a treat, announced it to her in grand and generous terms. So she was immediately suspicious. Such a gift was too out of character for her thrifty, steadfast parents. It only raised the stakes of her anxiety. "I think I'll stay home," she had said. But her father had ignored her, and her mother was too weak to do anything but stroke her hair and say, "Oh, Clare, think of the ocean."

As the date for her leave-taking approached, Clare had thrown books at the wall between her room and the room where her mother napped for long periods of each day. At bedtime, Clare sobbed into her pillow, vowing not to go but to chain herself to the oak tree that grew by the kitchen deck.

"Clare," Dad had said on the worst night, standing over her bed with his hands knotted up so tightly that his knuckles were white. "You have to learn to control your feelings. You're old enough now."

"How come you don't cry?" she had accused him.

After a long minute, he told her, "It doesn't do you any good to carry on. And it only makes it harder on Mom."

"I can't leave her," Clare said. "What if . . ."

"It's better you go," he preempted. "Better for you. Mom and I agree."

But Clare wasn't sure her mother did agree. The day Clare was to leave for the airport, her mother got up for breakfast and rubbed blusher onto her cheeks. The pink makeup over her pale skin looked like a clown's paint. Her voice was bright too, ringing falsely. Still, Clare kept watching her mother as she moved the food around on her plate. She couldn't take her eyes off her. *What if? What if?*

Her mother was staring out the bay window at the birds on

the feeder when Clare carried her suitcase downstairs. "Bye, Mom," she said, bending to kiss her.

"Have a good time, dear," her mother said sunnily. "Give my love to Aunt Fran." She never turned her head to look fully at Clare. In fact, she turned away, returned her gaze to the birds.

Aunt Fran was her mother's sister. Clare knew her only from occasional family Christmases and the rare summer reunion. Fran had married a navy airman, Uncle Tig, who was gruff and tight with his tongue and deceptively hale-chested. As a pilot, he had flown all over the world until a faulty coronary valve grounded him, and then he was too heartbroken to go far from his last base in Brunswick, Maine. He spoke little. In fact, when he picked Clare up at the airport in Boston and drove the five hours north, he said exactly eight words. "Let me get that," about her bag, and later when her stomach growled, "Fran is making supper." That was that.

Fran had written home to her sister that Tig's only solace since leaving the military was gardening, which didn't seem manly enough work at all—until Clare saw him do it. He hoisted out roots with a tractor and double-dug beds with a pickax and hauled in truckloads of stinking seaweed and manure and fish bones. He had taught himself the chemistry of soil and sun and water, and had coaxed up an Eden in the yard of his little cape. With his garden as his sole recommendation, one of the old summer families on the Hill had come to Tig and asked him to be caretaker at their estate.

The Prentisses of Manhattan and Sky Hill lived almost in the Atlantic, so far out on the peninsula was their summer place. It was called Last Look, and the house stood on a knoll that dropped on one side through tumbled boulders to the sea. On the other side, it was lapped by gardens that cascaded downhill and then finally trickled off into paths winding into the pine groves and birch woodlands that stretched for some ninety acres. Nestled at the edge of the woods was the caretaker's cottage, which was made of the same round rocks that had gone into the low wall surrounding the estate. Even this cottage had large windows and rooms that were cool and spacious under low ceilings. Its woodwork was carved. Its fireplace was deep. And there were two Ionic columns between the front parlor and the dining room. The Prentisses had always been generous with what they called "their people."

The evening Clare had arrived to stay in the gable room upstairs at the caretaker's cottage, the Prentisses had sent down a plate of gingersnaps from their kitchen and asked to have Clare come up the next morning, "after her journey had worn off." Tig had smirked when his wife read the note aloud, and Clare had asked, "What? What?"

"Nothing," Aunt Fran had said, at which Tig smirked again.

Clare had pressed, and her aunt had finally smiled and said, "Mrs. Prentiss likes to take charge of every little detail."

"And I'm a detail?"

Aunt Fran had only grinned.

All that had made Clare anxious about meeting the family in the mansion. In her small midwestern hometown, no one was openly rich. That would be unseemly. In fact, when Clare had once lamented that her friend Penny was too poor even to get a twist cone at the Dairy Queen with the rest of the kids, her father had shaken his head and said, "Her granddaddy has more money squirreled away than probably anyone else in town." So having no direct experience with the wealthy and having formed her ideas about them solely on what she had seen on television and at the movies, Clare was surprised by the genuine flesh-and-blood version.

Mrs. Prentiss herself was not at all what Clare expected. True, the grounds of Last Look were kept as immaculately as her Great-Aunt Mabel's parlor back home, and true, the house itself was a marvel of fine fabrics and beveled glass and hand-oiled wood. Clare had never actually seen a wall painted red before. But Mrs. Prentiss did not fit the rest of the picture. She usually wore a lavender sweater that was soiled on the elbows and unraveling at the left wrist, and her blond hair was short and curled around her ears in a mussed way. She did wear pearl stud earrings, but this one elegance was offset by shabby shorts and canvas sneakers. Often, Mrs. Prentiss climbed around on the shore rocks or rowed herself across the cove in a dinghy or went tramping through the woods, and most always, she had a book with her. She "ate books for breakfast, lunch, and dinner," her husband was fond of saying, and when Mrs. Prentiss found out that Clare also loved to read, she mentioned her name to the librarian in town, who soon hired the girl to shelve books and paste in card pockets and look after the children during story hour on Wednesday afternoons. Then, so Clare could easily get herself to the job, Mrs. Prentiss loaned her a red bicycle outgrown by a granddaughter named Elizabeth who was touring Europe that summer.

The ride back up the promontory road and into the village was two miles and much too short for Clare. She had never seen the ocean before coming to Maine. Now, every day, it was to her left and to her right as she pedaled inland off the narrow point. The water glittered through the trees. She could smell it, taste the salt in its perpetual gusts, and there was hardly a day going home, when she came to the rock bridge that ran across an incised cove, that she could resist stopping for a minute and sitting with her legs hanging over the side. It was a good place to think, there with her eyes looking deep into the clear water or far out to sea, where she could see the fringed islands knobbing up green.

There on the bridge, she thought about her mother, picked out a memory and concentrated on bringing it back in all detail: Mom standing over the range wearing only her bra and cutoff jeans because it was summer and she was canning pickles. The water bubbled like notes of music around the jars in the enamel kettle, and Mom hummed "Oklahoma"—except when she scorched her fingers and spat out a "damn." And when Clare crawled out of the shade of the kitchen table and laid her cheek against her mother's tanned thigh, the skin was cool and smooth and solid. The skin smelled like rising bread dough.

That was what she had been thinking about when she met Riley. "One shove and you're over," he said, coming up behind her in a red and rusted pickup truck that was so old it was all humps and had no straight edges or angles. He let it idle, smoking out its tailpipe.

"I love the water," she told him, trying to be sunny but strong. Right off, she didn't trust the look of him, though she did admire it. He had a narrow face, thickly freckled, and red hair that coiled from a cowlick into curls above his forehead. He was thin, but wound with muscle. His shoulders showed, taut and knotted and mottled brown as polished oak, under his sleeveless tee shirt. It was an undershirt really. She was noticing this when he stuck his hand out the window of his truck and pushed her over the side of the low bridge.

The water closed like sharpest winter around her, and when she came up, Riley had come down the side of the embankment. He was laughing, with his hands stuck nonchalantly into the back pockets of his jeans.

"You're lucky it's high tide," she said, heading for the other bank, away from him. She felt slapped all over, and her skin was as red as if someone had struck her repeatedly. "You could've killed me on the rocks."

This made him laugh all the harder.

⟶

"The postcard was from Riley, from *the* Riley Brackett, the one you . . . ?" JoJo cocked an eyebrow suggestively. By now she had finished eating her sushi and had both her hands wrapped around her cup of steaming green tea. She was leaning into the story, her interest heightened by a name she had heard years earlier on late nights when, unable to sleep, she and Clare had talked from their separate futons on the floor. They had amused one another with the stories of their lives, a practice that had since become a necessity.

"Would you listen?" Clare said. She took a bite of her maki combination. She still had four pieces of Boston roll left and three of the spicy tuna. She hadn't touched the tamago. She'd hardly had time to swallow.

"Was it?" JoJo pressed.

Clare shook her head no. But she couldn't speak. She was having trouble gaining control over a mouthful of maki.

JoJo groaned, impatient.

Coming in on the train today, Clare had felt that she would detonate before she could tell JoJo what had been happening. And yet now she enjoyed making Jo wait as she herself had waited for this chance to talk. She hung on for a few more suspenseful seconds before washing the mouthful of food down with some tea.

Then she recalled for her friend how she had been standing in her little house on the Hudson seventeen years later and how she could still hear Riley's laughter. "I'll be walking through an airport and think I hear it, you know? Or if I'm that kind of flu-sick where the fever makes your own head talk to you, then I'll hear him sometimes."

"Your own head talks to you when you've got a fever?"

"It sings too," Clare said. "And it sounds like it's on psychedelics, all wavery and liquid."

JoJo laughed but waved Clare on in her story. She was waiting. "Go on. Go on."

"And so I turned over the postcard, and there's his name: Riley Brackett. The words jump out at me. His name. It says, 'You don't know me, but I'm Riley Brackett's wife.'"

JoJo gasped. "His wife?"

⎯ᴐᴐ⎯

Holding the postcard closer, Clare had moved over into the light of the window to read more. The handwriting was in pencil and was carved deep into the glossy card, deliberate in every stroke. *You don't owe him anything*, it said. *Everybody knows that, after what he put you through. But there's been an accident, a bad one.*

Not another, Clare had thought. Not another.

He keeps asking for you, the note continued. *Nobody can do a thing with him. It's none of your business, I know, but could you come see him?* It was signed, *Sincerely, Laurie Brackett.*

Then there was a postscript squeezed in at the bottom. The post office had laid down a code sticker over it, obscuring the words. Clare worked her nail under one edge and pulled the sticker free. *We have two kids. It would mean a lot to them.*

Clare had let the screen door slap closed behind her as she went out onto the porch. The steps were in the sunshine, and she sat on the top one, still holding the postcard. Feeling had crept into her nerve endings as she read the cryptic note, had moved along the surface of her skin and deep into the muscles of her arms. She didn't know what it was she felt.

⎯ᴐᴐ⎯

JoJo shuddered and said, "How awful.... But what a bizarre thing for somebody's wife to do, don't you think?"

Clare shrugged. "I didn't know what to think. I mean, I was sorry, of course. I thought it was terrible for him and for his family. And I was a little curious, you know, about the specifics."

"Of course," JoJo said. "It was so cryptic."

Clare tried to think of a way to explain. Before that postcard came, it had been years since she had thought of her summer in Maine. It had been easier not to think of it. Her mother had been dying, after all. And Clare herself had almost died that terrible night of the eclipse. So after the summer was over and she was back home, it had been easier not to think of what had happened to her there—for better and for worse. It had been easier not to look back. Still, she had felt a sudden gratitude that someone had remembered. It was not lost, not entirely. Riley had kept it. "I was touched," she told JoJo, "that he remembered. It was a long time ago."

"Still, touched or not," JoJo said, "you wouldn't consider going? I mean that would be completely eerie." She looked hard at Clare. "Wouldn't it?"

"Of course," Clare said. "That's exactly what I thought. How could I go waltzing into Riley Brackett's life after all these years, especially knowing that it was a terrible time for his family? Plus they were all strangers to me, even him. I couldn't. I mean I could see I was merely some last straw his wife was grasping at."

"I'm sensing a *but* here...."

Clare sighed. "But ..."

"Omigod, Clare, you didn't, did you?" JoJo put both palms flat on the table as if to steady herself. "I can't believe this. I finally break down and get married, take my first vacation in six years, go on a honeymoon in Africa, and you meanwhile are the one having the adventure."

"I should've asked you more about it, Jo. I'm sorry. Did you bring pictures of the albino elephant?"

JoJo clamped her with a severe look. There would be no swerving off subject. "When do we get to that *but?*" she demanded.

"It was because of Michael," Clare said.

"Michael?" JoJo looked at her for a measuring minute, then reached for her famously overstuffed purse, which was really more of a gym duffel. She began to rummage.

"What are you doing?"

JoJo held up her cell phone in explanation. She began punching in numbers. "I'm deputizing Jennifer to hold down the fort this afternoon."

"Why?" Clare asked, then lapsed into silence as JoJo chirped instructions into the phone, choreographing her own absence from the office. When Clare had first met JoJo, through a "roommate wanted" ad in the network newsletter, JoJo had found it necessary to set five alarms just to get up in the morning. She hadn't seemed to know what three of the food groups were. And she had owned a wardrobe that consisted of six pairs of Nikes, two pairs of black leggings, and her father's cast-off Brooks Brothers shirts. Now, all these years later, though she still smacked her strawberry Bubble-Yum, JoJo had evolved into the most powerful executive producer at the network. She was in charge of the prime-time news show that always pulled in the most Emmys, and she could pretty much do as she wanted. But one thing had not changed: her standard for what friendship deserved.

"Okay," JoJo said, as she snapped the phone closed. "Let's go for a walk in the park."

"Jo," Clare protested. "You're snowed under...."

"You need to talk," JoJo said. "And I wouldn't be able to concentrate if I went back to the office without hearing this. Do you really think you can just drop this on me and then walk away?" She snorted.

Before Clare could shrug it off, JoJo had signed the credit card slip with a scrawl, slung her purse over her shoulder, and opened the door to the humid breath of summer in the city. On the sidewalk, she unwrapped a piece of bubble gum for herself and another for Clare.

Taking the gum, Clare thought that this was what she had counted on. She had counted on JoJo to understand what she needed now, just as she had last year, when Clare had seen no way of helping herself, and JoJo had known to make a vat of cookie dough and sit with her through hours of "Nickelodeon." "Laugh," JoJo had instructed her sternly on those dark, scary days. And Clare had always found a way to obey.

Now, JoJo blew a big bubble and popped it. Having thus determined that her gum was chewed to the right consistency, she cued Clare. "Okay," she said, "it was because of Michael...." Then she waited for Clare to begin.

Later on the day the postcard arrived, a hot sogginess crept in. All afternoon it came, reminding Clare of the fog coming in off the ocean in Maine. Some evenings that long-ago summer, she and Riley had watched strands of fog move among the little shingled houses and up the streets of the quiet seaside village, purposeful as ghosts. Riley had told her then that his Granny Mead had believed the fog peeked in at her window and took word of her fidelity back to her husband on board his ship, the *Molly*. Sometimes, Riley's grandmother told him, the fog also brought to land the news of someone lost at sea. Once, on a foggy night when she was a young mother, Granny Mead had doubled into tears over her pudding, despairing for her husband's life. And it was true, her premonition. He had been washed overboard in a Gulf Stream storm.

Clare hadn't thought of the story in years, but as the sun went down over the Hudson and she sat on the porch eating a supper of Havarti cheese and crackers, she noticed how the humidity was hung like smudged, sodden gauze over the river valley. It looked like fog. And it did look too as though it might bear tidings, and certainly nothing of comfort.

She sat outside until the fireflies had sparked in the grass and had begun to rise. Then she went to her bed. The peepers throbbed beyond the screens, and before it grew too late, the lights of an occasional car looked in the window, scanned her bedroom, and were gone. She sat in stillness under nothing but a cotton sheet, and the only movement came from the fan blowing. She was reading, waiting for Michael. But some minute, it took no longer than a single minute, she lost hold on herself, began to sink, began to let sleep rise up around her and then over her.

Riley was lying in the pine needles, and she was covering him with them, strand by strand. "Do you love me?" he asked. And she laughed. "Do you love me?" he asked again. "Clare, do you?" She put the needles on his forehead, where it was freckled. She laid them in the seam of his bare abdomen where the fine runnel of hair was red as cinnamon.

"You should love me," he said, "because I love the backs of your knees and the moons of your fingernails and the tips of your eyelashes where they turn blond."

"Hush," she told him, and laid pine needles on his mouth, covered his eyes.

"Hush," he told her in answer, and rose toward her and turned over on top of her so that the pine needles were coming down on her like autumn and he was above her and his lips were on hers, and she could feel the heat of him and the hard fact of how he loved her, the immutability of it. She was afraid he would swallow her. She wanted him to swallow her. She wanted to slide down into him, dissolve there and run in his blood, look through his eyes, savor her own kisses off his tongue. She wanted. She wanted. She wanted. She ached with how she wanted. "You love me," he told her.

⟶ℭℭ⟶

Her bedstand light was still burning when she jolted back to herself. The cordless phone on the other pillow bleated again. "Michael?" she said into the receiver.

"Hi, sweet girl," he said. It was just after midnight, and his voice was grave with exhaustion. She could hear the physical strain in his vocal cords and knew that she was another of his obligations. Before he could sleep, he had to call her.

"How's your mother?" she asked, propping herself higher on the pillows. She struggled to get back to this moment, to return to her husband.

"No better, no worse," he answered, then sighed.

Limbo, Clare thought, and it was loud in her head. *She's in limbo. And as long as she's there, so are we.* But she didn't say this to him. She'd said it before. She'd said too many things. For his mother, there was only one way out of limbo. There was no going back to being Mommy Belle, the woman who had cut heart shapes into her son's toast every morning and sewed curtains for every room in her house as well as the house next door, the woman who made the "floatiest" matzoh balls on the face of the earth. After this, there was only one choice left for Belle: not being at all.

Clare bit the word *limbo* in two without saying it and groped for something simple but full of understanding. Lately though, she couldn't understand, couldn't fall into place with her husband's emotions, couldn't remember how. And how could that be? How could it have happened? This was the man whose emotions had been her mirror, the man who had sat on the couch with her one Friday night watching televised reports about troops coming home from the Gulf War. Neither of them had believed in killing for oil fields. Neither of them even knew anyone in the military. But as Clare was trying to conceal the feelings that were brimming in her eyes, she heard sniffling, and there he was over there, grinning sheepishly at his own soft heart while tears coursed down into the rough stubble of his evening beard: crying over a father reunited with a little girl in ponytails; over a bride kissing her earnest soldier; over a uniformed mother coming home to a teenage son who lifted her off the ground in his enthusiasm.

"The dance," Clare had called it, that way she and Michael had of reacting in unison. They had moved smoothly together: his hand on the small of her back as they skirted a slow walker on a city sidewalk; her eyes on the map before he knew the road he was driving on would split up ahead; his hand closing around hers just at the point in the movie when the heartbreak tightened around her throat. Whenever she had rolled over in the night, his arms were already opening for her.

Now she felt how badly they jerked out of step with one another. She got ahead; he lagged. She reached for words that would signal her sympathy; he lapsed into silence. They hesitated. They stepped on each other's toes.

She missed the dance. She missed him. And not just because he was away in Massachusetts. Even when he was home, part of him was gone, worrying over his mother or talking late into the night on the phone with his aunt Del, who cared for Belle every day, or at least did her best to care for her. Day after day, Michael turned the crisis this way and that in his mind. It was like some kind of conceptual puzzle to him, a mental Rubic's cube that he examined late at night by the circular glow of his desk lamp just as he examined it by the dim first light that fell through their bedroom window in the morning.

When Clare opened her eyes most days, his were already open, staring at the dusk that clung in the corners of their room. "Michael," she would whisper, putting her hand in the dark nest of hair on his chest, and he would seem not to hear her nor to feel her touch. Minutes later he would shudder to consciousness and pick up her hand and kiss her wrist just there where her pulse beat. Even as his lips brushed her skin, his breath warm, even then Clare felt nothing except cold, certain dread.

Clare had thought she could prevent the worst from happening to her. Not death. She could face that, she thought. She could face just not being. But she couldn't face loss. She had barely survived losing her mother. She had survived her mother's death only because of her father's work ethic: *Toil will save you.* She believed in it. She desperately believed in it.

The autumn after her mother's death, Clare's father had gone back into his firm and insisted on spearheading the design for a new corporate headquarters in Minneapolis. He had worked twenty-hour days in exhausting succession. But at least the fatigue muted the grief. Clare had missed him and needed him. Still, she couldn't blame him. She was finding her own salve in devoting long hours to the editorship of the school newspaper, which won a national award her senior year, her season of deepest mourning.

Ever since, she had never been happier than when she was working. When she was working, she wasn't scared. When she was working, she was doing everything in her power to keep herself safe from loss. Bad things happened only when you left yourself open to them, when you got lax or lazy, when you turned to see what was behind you when you should've been focused ahead, looking toward your goal. Wasn't that what her dad had always told her? "Don't catch trouble's eye," he had cautioned.

Maybe she had looked over her shoulder and caught trouble's eye. Or maybe it had caught hers. She knew the day it had happened, the day last spring when she'd squeezed in a checkup with the gynecologist after flying in from doing a series of on-camera interviews in D.C. It had been a harried day, and a dozen times she had considered canceling with the doctor in New York and taking a later shuttle so she could do one more interview, so she could set up one more shot under the boughs of the blossoming cherry trees.

It had been the day the cherry petals started turning loose in pink showers, a beautiful soft blue day. Sometimes since, she had thought the rogue cells might not have taken root in her body if she had not taken notice of them, if she had not acknowledged their presence, if she had just stayed and done her job. If she had stayed and worked, pushed harder. If she had stayed and worked longer in the wafting petals, in the last long light of a spring day.

ᐦᨏ

"Are you okay?" she asked Michael now.

"Sure," he said. But the word was more sigh than anything made of the hard alphabet.

She waited for him to elaborate, waited for him to tell her what it was like to coax his agitated mother out of her clothes, to wrestle her arms free of the couch cushion she insisted on carrying for security, what it was like to hold her under the spray of water and to sponge the sharp ridge along her spine, what it was like to talk to her as she had talked to him when he was a toddler in the kitchen sink with a soap beard and sudsy pointed ears and a peaked little elf's cap of bubbles. Mommy Belle had always kept that snapshot over her kitchen sink, where she could see it when she washed the supper dishes. "Our little elf," she had called him.

Clare had actually seen her mother-in-law kiss that picture in its frame. But the last time Clare had been to Belle's house, the image was gloomy with dust and soap spatters. Clare could hardly make out Michael's crooked little grin.

She wondered if Michael thought of reciprocity when he dried between the blades of his mother's shoulders, under her arms. She wondered if he remembered how his mother had looked at him with gray eyes that loved him best and if he twinged to see those same eyes turned on him now without any warmth of recognition, but instead with wariness. Whose hands were these that touched her with such intimacy? Who was this stranger whose palms rubbed her with Johnson's good, sweet powder?

On her end of the phone line, Clare lay under the light sheet and waited for Michael to give part of his burden to her, for him to open the door that would let her inside with him. She had waited a long time now. But Michael had not let her in. Maybe it was an impossibility: He could not let her inside his ordeal. This belonged only to him.

Even as she knew how selfish—and foolish—it was to resent his privacy, she did. She did so with her whole heart. It wasn't just resentment, though. It was terror. She was afraid of losing him. She was afraid of losing more of him than she had already relinquished. There had been a time when she believed him to be all that she had searched for, all she had needed: something to last.

She had met him because her executive producer had sent her downtown to do a piece on alternative art. It was just about the time that chocolate nudity erupted into a debate over government funding of the arts, and Clare's job was to capture the color of the avant-garde scene where some taxpayer money would inevitably go. This was drudgery for her. She was sorry. She had nothing against any of the contortions people wanted to put themselves through to make art. It just happened that she preferred Mostly

Mozart and Lincoln Center, or some bruised and blazing saxophone at Michael's Pub. Her taste in art ran to the Italian cherub paintings at the Met. So sue her. She was young and single and had no use for hip. Not that she didn't wear the opaque black tights and the same little Lycra skirt that everyone else wore, it was just that she dressed it up with a high-collar lace blouse from the vintage basement on Columbus. She sometimes added what might have been her grandmother's old brooches—except that she had bought them for fifty cents apiece at the Sunday street fair. "Nostalgia chic," JoJo quipped.

In the context of the garage-style performance space on Varick Street, Clare McClendon looked out of place—she was wearing Victorian-style button boots and a crocheted dickey that night—and Michael Kline looked as though he had stepped naturally out of the shadows of the nearby buildings, which leaned over the street with no light coming from their barred, grimy windows. He had a nip of goatee on his chin, and his forehead was high and smooth, his hairline having already started its retreat. He was dressed in smug black and was wearing conspicuously gratuitous sunglasses. Dark and handsome and mysterious had never been her type. But he was playing the piano for a performance-art piece choreographed by his friend, Dane, who spun out blood-red mashed potatoes from under the tires of a Harley. And though Clare had no patience for the absurdity of the performance, she did feel that there was a limber lyricism to the music. This was the point, she found out later.

Michael always told people that he had wanted to marry Clare from the moment he saw her. "She had freckles on her nose," he would say. "Do you know how rare it is to find a fresh face in this city?" Fresh face or no, that night she had only wanted to get her reporting on tape and get back uptown. The only thing that won him her company was the pressing fact that she was dizzy with hunger, and he was offering to lead her to a special little Indian place on Sixth Street. "The best," he had assured her, and so she had sent her camera and sound men back uptown without her.

The entire street was lined with cheap Indian restaurants, but she never would have thought to eat there on her own. If she ate Indian food, it was on Fifty-seventh Street at an expense-account restaurant run by a Delhian movie star who wore her flower-color silks to greet guests. But as she and Michael walked down the row of restaurants and he recited the attributes of first one and then the next, she began to be drawn in by the idea. In the windows there were men swathed in white robes, playing sitars and drums. They sat on the heels of their long bare feet, endearingly, as children do, and their music sifted out onto the street with the spice of the curries. She began to feel as though she were somewhere only her passport could have taken her.

Michael's favorite restaurant was the size of a hallway and lit only with twinkling Christmas lights. Tables for two lined one wall, tables for four the other. Clare had to squeeze into her chair because it was back-to-back with a guy in a tuxedo who was toasting his buddy (or lover) with a bottle of Taj Mahal beer. Finally settled, she looked up to make some smart remark to Michael and found he had taken off his glasses. The words had dissolved on her tongue, and she was sure she had blushed. He had beautiful eyes. And, of all things, dimples.

"What's the matter?" he asked.

She had not told him, of course. They had talked instead of her work, and his. He played the piano at the Pierre, he admitted. Fifth Avenue. Uptown. She laughed. "And I thought you were so horrifically downtown."

Michael had explained that Dane had wanted to undercut the violence of his one-person, one-motorcycle diorama by employing the charm of piano music. But Dane had insisted that Michael wear the sunglasses—as a disguise. "Because of my eyes," Michael shrugged. "He claims my eyes are the size of a cow's." He told her that because of Dane, his college buddies all called him Bo, which was short for Bovine.

She laughed and agreed (though only to herself) that without a makeover, Michael would have ruined the edginess of Dane's performance. His eyes gave away his sweetness.

"So they dressed me for the part," he said, running his hand back through his hair.

"Down to that stuff on your chin?" she teased.

A flicker passed in his eyes. "That's all me," he said.

"Oh," she said. "It looks good on you." But the goatee was gone the next time she saw him, which was the night she first learned what he could do in a kitchen. He had made a wild mushroom fritatta, and also poppy-seed rolls that he said came from Thomas Jefferson's recipe. He had made her laugh that night too, and when she was eating her strawberries with balsamic vinegar, he leaned over and kissed her. "Sorry," he said after he had touched his lips to hers. "I couldn't help myself."

Again, she couldn't speak.

"You're beautiful," he said. "May I kiss you again?"

And she had nodded, and they had kissed, and he had never had to ask again. It had been a long time since anyone had cooked for her (other than JoJo's microwave popcorn). It had been a long time since anyone had taken her arm to guide her around dog poop on the sidewalk or held her hand as she was falling asleep. She had taken care of herself for so long that the relief surprised her, the relief of letting him share her life and its daily load.

When JoJo wasn't home, Clare and Michael shared Ivory liquid-soap bubble baths in the apartment's kitchen tub, or sat on the fire escape in the rain, or glowed together like embers on her futon mattress on the floor. In the afterglow, they would lie in one another's arms and describe the life they dreamed of having: No future was settled between them, but already they coordinated a fantasy. She told him what they would see from their bedroom window—trees and moving water—and he told her what he would make for breakfast on their fiftieth wedding anniversary. They named their someday dogs, calling them Fred and Ethel. They bandied about names for children. "Ezekiel, called Zeke," she would say. "Norman," he would counter.

On nights when JoJo was around, the three of them sprawled across the mattress and ate raw cookie dough out of the bowl while watching old Doris Day and Rock Hudson movies. JoJo hauled Clare into the bathroom one time, sat her down on the toilet, and whispered, "I'm sorry. But I've never met a man who would willingly watch a double feature of fluff plus hold his own with the cookie dough. He's perfect." Clare thought then that she loved Michael as much for making Jo happy as she loved him for making her happy.

"The Michael," JoJo called him, as in The Standard. "When I find my Michael," she would say, measuring her own expectations against him. "You can't take your eyes off her," JoJo teased him once, and he had shrugged and said, "Why should I?"

"Why should you!" JoJo had laughed. "Hear, hear."

On a night when everything went wrong—the doctor gave him the wrong prescription for his contacts, the taxi got a flat tire going through Central Park, the waiter was surly, and a downpour started a block before they got home—on that night, Michael asked Clare to marry him. After she had said yes, yes, and yes!, she had asked him why he had chosen this night. "It chose me," he said. "I just suddenly realized that if we could have fun even on a night like tonight, we could get through anything. Somehow."

She had believed that too. It was in every yes she had given him, that belief in their ability to get through anything together. In him she found what was necessary: someone who could let her have her strength and keep his own. Someone to knit her resolve to, double it. She had thought that together they were a barrier against anything. Impervious to flat tires and sudden rain, as well as sadness and loss.

They were not. They merely loved each other.

And she knew they still loved each other. But as she kept the tears on her cheek from seeping into her voice and as they continued talking past each other in the June midnight, far apart and linked only by a vibrating wire, she also knew that they were vulnerable. They were vulnerable to all the worst things—to sadness, clearly, and loss, and every terrible thing she could imagine in the dark moments when she woke in the night, defenseless against her own fears. Their loving each other would not keep them from harm, could not. It would not seal them off from trouble, nor lift them above it. Hadn't they already caught trouble's eye?

Clare packed her bag without considering whether she should or should not go. She just knew she had to. Had to. She wasn't geared to sit still, to languish. Michael knew that as well as anyone. One early rainy morning, when they were vacationing in a cabin on a Vermont mountainside, Michael had rolled over to see her tying on her hiking sneakers. "What are you doing?" he had asked sleepily. "The chanterelles might be popping," she had said, and he had covered his eyes with the long of his arm and said, "Clare, you really can't have fun unless it's work." And she had laughed on her way out the door, but he was right.

The months just passed in California, though grueling, had been an odd respite for her. Her worries had been suspended lightly in the taut wires of her work and consequently had been no burden to her. And though she had been glad to look out the plane window and see New York stacked like child's blocks between the two rivers, and though it had been a pleasure to drive through the springtime countryside and home to the cottage where Michael had kept up with her garden while she was away, she felt lost being home now. Without him here, even her flowers were no distraction.

Away covering the trial, she had missed the crocuses blooming among the twisted roots of the old maple tree, and also the daffodils, and all but the latest tulips. Over the phone, she would ask, "Is the *Fritillaria meleagris* blooming yet?"

And he would say, "Describe that."

"Like a little lantern," she'd say. "It's checkered."

"Purple and white are both up," he'd confirm.

The last deep purple lilac was in full bloom the day Michael had turned into their driveway, bringing her home from the airport. And when she had stepped out into the air and breathed in the scent of the lilac, she had felt such a sense of well-being that she had grabbed Michael around the neck and kissed his eyelids until he had finally dropped her bags and wrapped his arms around her so hard that her feet came off the ground. "Welcome home, sweet girl," he had said.

"Good to be here," she had whispered into his ear before taking the lobe into her mouth and tasting his skin again. And she had meant it. Being home felt good.

The next day they had gone to JoJo's May wedding at the rambling beach house in Jersey, and they had drunk too much champagne and then danced it off until the sun rose red out of the Atlantic. When Clare had kissed the bride goodbye, Jo had said, "You look happy." And Clare had realized on the drive home that she was starting to remember how it could feel, being happy, and that realization had enfolded her for a few days, for the few days when she had not had to be anywhere but with Michael. And he had not had to be anywhere but with her.

They made love in the mornings as May days lengthened into June's, tenderly relearning their way around each other. Afterward, Michael brewed café latte and brought it back to her in bed, and later, when they had roused themselves, they walked most days to the French bakery and came home to the porch with croissants stretchy with sweet butter. In the afternoons, he took the train into the city to work, and she crawled around among the flowers, talking to them as she pulled the weeds out from between their toes. "Doesn't that feel better," she'd say from under the brim of her floppy straw hat, and then she would get a mental image of herself that amused her so much that she had to lie back in the shiny-bladed grass and look at the clouds and laugh at herself. That laughter was a prayer. It was full of gratitude.

When Michael made it home in time for late dinners, she had lighted the candles on the porch and brought out platters of roasted fish or grilled chicken with lemon and garlic. Michael had poured the wine, the good Chablis they had found in France two years before, and she had thought more than once—had allowed herself to hope—that maybe her luck had turned again, had serpentined back round. And when Michael had asked if she had a good day, she was able to lift her glass and look in his eyes, and say with conviction, "Yes, I had a good day."

Then Mommy Del had called. Clare had answered the phone one Sunday, and Del had said, "Oh, Clare," as though hers was the most unexpected voice Del could possibly hear. That tone of Del's always made Clare feel like an interloper in her own home.

Taking the cordless phone, Michael had closed the door to the little study, and after that Clare could hear no more than the baritone hum of his voice punctuated by pauses. Afterward, his eyes were clouded over, but when she asked how things were in River Port, he only said, "The same."

Clare had gone out to her garden then, stung by her exclusion. But watering didn't soothe her, and when she had come in again, she found that Michael had helped with the laundry. She sighed at the discovery, and he said, "What?" And she said, "Nothing." But she meant, how could he have washed both white piles together, not the delicates separately as she had intended? When he figured out his mistake, he berated himself for not having asked, and then she berated herself for not just appreciating his help, and they walked tiptoe orbits around each other's feelings the rest of the day, intimate strangers.

From the beginning of their marriage, Clare had felt like a stranger in Michael's family. But now, even from such a long distance, his family was more and more often making her feel like a stranger in her own life. As a newlywed, she had told herself that the Klines would warm to her. But they never had. They were pleasant enough to her. It was just that she was always waiting for the pleasantness to wear off, for them to start feeling like family, like her family—flawed and comfortable and forgiving. Instead, they kept her in the parlor of their lives, and when something important or awkward had to be discussed or accomplished, Michael was siphoned off to the inner sanctum of the kitchen, and she was left with her legs crossed and her hands folded idly in her lap.

She blamed herself for this, as much as anyone. Soon after she and Michael became engaged, his mother had asked Michael what Clare would like to call them. "We thought it would be nice if she called us what you and your sister do," she suggested. But when Michael relayed this to Clare, she had said, "I had a mother, and I've got a dad. I can't call anyone else by their names."

Since then, when she was feeling worst about her failure as a daughter-in-law, she recalled her inflexibility on this point—and on others: not taking Michael's name but keeping her dad's, not calling Belle or Del when she had a question but calling Aunt

Fran instead. It was her own fault that the Klines treated her as an outsider. She should've just choked down her squeamishness in the beginning when they had asked for an affection she did not yet feel. Now it was too late.

JoJo always scoffed at these self-recriminations. "You can't win," she had often comforted Clare. "How can you win with *two* mothers-in-law? Count 'em, two. Most people don't survive the one."

Clare had counted them. Over and over. She had been intrigued when Michael first told her about his family: His mother, Belle, had an identical twin, Adele, called Del. At birth, their mother had rhymed them like poetry, and they had lived in synchrony ever since. They had gray eyes and ash-blond hair and brittle figures that made them look nervous. From childhood, they had dressed to match, first in playsuits and later in coordinating sweater sets and even in the same summer housedresses. They claimed that they did not consult each other about what to wear each day. They would just step out their front doors every morning reflecting in their very clothes how alike they were even in the solitude of their private minds. The only difference was that Belle wore shades of pink and Del wore purples, so babysitters and teachers and, later, boys could distinguish them one from the other.

In the end, the boys they met could tell them apart with no trouble. Jake and Ese Kline were also identical twins. Jake met Del in the grocery store and asked her out, but when he met her sister, he only had eyes for Belle. And it was a good thing because Ese thought Del was far superior to her twin.

These two couples had adored double-dating, and though they were a spectacle wherever they went, either it did not bother them or it secretly thrilled them. Michael was never sure. In any case, they were all of modest middle-class backgrounds and basically reserved. The men entered their father's dress-manufacturing business, and the women loved to bargain-hunt. And they never did anything outlandish—except to marry in a double-chuppah, double-ring ceremony and afterward to live in neighboring houses that appeared as though one was looking in a mirror at itself. Rhododendrons bloomed in unison, and brick walks wound up to yellow doors. Sheer drapes hung at the same sweep in the bay windows. Duplicate Ford four-doors sat in the driveways. And the children of these twin marriages, a boy and a girl born within days of one another, were raised as brother and sister. After all, the children were genetically siblings, as the parents were always quick to tell dentists and kindergarten teachers and school administrators. They just had two mommys and two daddys.

Michael had since counted himself blessed for this quirk—and not because of any superfluity of parents. No matter how much things appeared to be the same from sister to sister and brother to brother, there were imbalances. Shortcomings were compensated for by the other twin's strengths, and together Belle and Del, Jake and Ese just about added up to one mom and one dad. Belle was as competent at homemaking as Del was incompetent. Del was as lively and fun-loving as Belle was steady and serious. Michael could remember Mommy Del falling from an apple tree and tipping over canoes and always laughing about her mishaps. He could remember Mommy Belle solemnly patching up his scraped knees and holding cool washrags on his head when he had the flu. And Pop Ese was as good at making a living as Jake was incapable of it. While Jake taught Michael how to fly-fish gracefully and how to build birdhouses, Ese taught him how to save his allowance and balance his checkbook. Belle and Jake may have lived at 126 Missouri Avenue and Del and Ese may have lived at 128, but their resources—financial and emotional—were pooled, out of necessity and loyalty and what they would've called love, if they had been the kind of people to name anything that they felt.

This unique universe, self-contained and self-sustaining, did not need Clare. The Klines had the comfort of each other and operated as though they had no need of anything—or anyone—outside the picket fences of their side-by-side houses. And so it did not turn out to be what Clare had hoped when, in the first blush of her love for Michael, she first heard about it. Being an only child, she had always wanted to marry into a big family, where conversation was loud around the Thanksgiving table and a Fourth of July required two watermelons. But this was not at all the kind of big family she was inheriting. First of all, the daughter, Kathleen, was so estranged by her upbringing that she had shortened her name to Kate and had moved halfway across the country to avoid the obligation of coming home for anything more than the rare family holiday. When, to her chagrin, Kate had given birth to identical twin girls, she named them Amethyst and Zoe, and alternately dressed one in bright plaids and the other in pastel ruffles. She wanted nothing to pass from one generation to another, other than the propensity for having twins, which she clearly had no control over.

After a while, Clare couldn't help but see Kate's point. Around Belle's dinner table, the twin couples ate every evening at precisely five-forty-five. They each had one glass of wine, a California cabernet sauvignon that was bought by the case and stacked in the cellar at 126. Any dinner conversation was regarding the food, and this was usually limited to a single comment, which began to sound like an echo because they each seemed to repeat it not quite before the previous person had finished the sentence. "You've outdone yourself now, Belle," Ese would say to his sister-in-law; then Jake would pick it up; then Del. And Belle would say something demure in answer, usually to the tune of, "Well, Del picked the blueberries." And then the echo would begin again. "What a lovely idea, Del. *What a lovely idea. . . . What a lovely . . .* "

After dinner, there was coffee in the living room, and then Del and Ese stepped out of Belle and Jake's back door, crossed the

driveways, and went into their own back door. From angled re-
cliners, everyone watched the eleven o'clock news through the
weather report, but by eleven-thirty both houses were dark. Clare
felt guilty even burning her bedside lamp late to read, but she
could never fall asleep without a few chapters of a book. Michael
snickered at her because she always spoke in a whisper at his
parents' house, so wary was she of stumbling afoul of the formal
day-in, day-out waltz of the Klines and Klines.

Michael teased her about it, but she noticed that he didn't exactly speak up himself. Though he had always been able to joke
about his family's quirks when he was warmed up over some wine
at a little bistro in the city, he went right along with the dance
when he was there in River Port, validating what his mothers and
his fathers all expected him to validate. His sister's rejection may
have caused the parents a misstep or two, may have caused them
to veer from their graceful certainty into some shadow of doubt
about their parallel existence, but Michael loved them too much
to do anything but fall in with them: one two three four; if they
needed them, of course he would go. One two three four.

_⌒⌒_

Clare set the timers to water her gardens, and while she was out
there, she cut a bouquet for Michael, bright and garish, the way
he liked a palette. "Jazzy," he'd say. "Very Coltrane." She put in
extra sweet peas for their perfume and then wrapped the whole
thing up with the stems set in a plastic cup of water to keep them
fresh.

In her imagination, she saw herself pulling up in front of his
parents' house in River Port. She saw Michael coming around the
corner of the house, carrying a ladder. He would be dressed in his
faded overalls, the ones that were torn at the knee, and he would

have his Apple computer baseball cap turned backward on his head. His eyebrows would be pulled into a knot over his brow, and his big eyes would look darker, solemn. And then he would see her, and he would quicken his step and come to her and loop an arm around her waist so that her whole body would kink when he drew her to him.

But even as she wedged the bouquet into the front floorboard of the Saturn with the picnic basket and her handbag, she twinged with doubt. Maybe Michael wouldn't want her help. Wasn't that the pivot of the whole matter? This trouble with Mommy Belle had only made the Klines withdraw further into their insularity, drawing Michael along with them.

Jake and Ese had died soon after Clare had married Michael, and that is when she had begun to see how differently the twins lived in the world. On the golf course, Ese had a massive and fatal heart attack, and days later, Jake went in his sleep, like one of those surviving spouses Clare had read about: He was killed by grief. They were only in their fifties, but even on the afternoon of the funeral, Belle had insisted that Jake couldn't bear to live without Ese, and why should he? As if to prove that point, in the months and years that followed, the widows' devotion to one another intensified: Belle cleaned 126, then crossed the yard to clean 128; all the while, Del hung in her shadow like a trout nosing its favorite rock. And when Del began her yardwork, in the cool of the long shadows after supper, Belle followed her around.

It was easy for Michael to say—and believe—that his "mothers" were only becoming more alike as they aged: "Soon no one will be able to tell us apart, if this keeps up," Del had teased him. "Not even you." Belle began to keep house like Del. At first she only left dishes in her sink or ignored a soap ring in the tub, but eventually she was putting away leftovers in the dishwasher or wandering around the backyard singing "God Bless America" in a hoarse alto.

"Something is wrong," Clare had told Michael driving home after one visit, and she had seen on his face that he knew it. But he had kept his eyes on the road and said, "No, it's just the way they are. All their lives they've been each other more than they've been themselves, you know? And now that they're getting older, the lines are really blurring."

Clare had felt rebuffed for having spoken up.

Then, sometime later, when she and Michael had been invited up to celebrate his birthday, they arrived to find Del in the kitchen, chopping vegetables. Del had never wielded a kitchen knife in her whole life—for good reason. Her fingers were too uncertain to execute delicate work. Pruning shears suited her better. "Belle's teaching me how to cook," she said gaily. But Belle was only walking around, opening the refrigerator or turning on the tap water for no reason. Clare had said, "Here, let me bail you out there, Del," but this had been the wrong thing to say. It hadn't been playing along with their ruse that everything was as it should be. Del had sewn her mouth into a puckered straight line and simply ignored the request, ignored Clare's very presence.

Afterward, at the supper table, Belle had tried to eat her chicken with the blunt backside of her knife. She had set her wine glass down in her soup bowl. She had burped out loud. And no one else at the table had missed a beat. One two three four, one two three four.

In bed that night, after despairing that Michael would ever broach the subject himself, Clare had rolled over and laid her arm across his stomach and asked, "Did anybody else notice that there was a black hole in the dining room tonight?" And he had sighed.

Looking back, Clare regretted saying it. She didn't mean that his mother was a black hole. But Belle had a disease, and that disease seemed to absorb all the normalcy, all the honesty, all the energy in the room. It seemed voracious, destroying even the things that bound them to each other: mother to child, sister to sister, husband to wife. And Clare seemed to be the only one able to acknowledge it.

To this day, she had never heard anybody in the family say the name of the disease out loud, though by now they were all aware of what it was. Belle herself was past naming her affliction before it was even diagnosed, but Clare had never heard Del say it either, though she knew that Del must sometimes have had to make the utterance. After all, Del had spent months and then years calling doctors all over the country and, failing to find what she needed from them, calling healers all over the world. She was looking for a way—any way—to save her sister: through strange black herbs from China, or blood-boiling techniques in Mexico, or break-through pharmaceuticals out of Holland that somebody might smuggle to her in the toe of a shoe. She wanted to save Belle. Maybe, Clare thought, it was the only way Del knew to save herself.

Staying over one night, Clare had woken in the dead still of night to see a shadow looming over her. It was a blackness darker than the night around it. And, in the instant she had opened her eyes to it, she had screamed. Michael had bolted out of his sleep and reached for the light, but it was only Mommy Belle standing there with her nightgown on inside out and her face slack. Harmless. Del came stumbling into the room. "What is it?" she cried.

"She scared me," Clare stammered. "I woke up and she was there. . . ."

Del had wrapped her arm around her sister's shoulder, and she had looked at Clare with lashing eyes. "How could you scream at her that way?" she had said. "She didn't mean anything." She had led her twin away, and Clare had turned to Michael, the tears already stinging in her eyes, but he had only said, "Why did you have to scream like that, Clare?" And she had known without saying it that it would win her no sympathy to say she had been asleep and then had been confused and frightened. It would win

her no sympathy. She had screamed out in terror, not at her
mother-in-law, but at what a disease had done to her mother-in-
law. And the Klines didn't understand that. To them, she was
screaming at someone they loved.

Not even Michael would say the name of the disease, not even
after it had been diagnosed as an early onset of what they most
feared, not even after he had gone with his mothers to specialists
who asked Belle what day of the week it was and who was pres-
ident now. So when Clare let the word slip out in her own con-
versations with Michael, she felt that she was firing a bullet at
him. He invariably flinched. "Sorry," she would amend herself
immediately. "Sorry." But when she was alone in the shower with
the most unhappy of her moods, she muttered in loud hostility at
the terrible black hole that was swallowing their lives, the black
hole that was consigning them each and all to a void, destroying
them slowly, one synapse at a time, year after long, long year:
"Alzheimer's, Alzheimer's, ravening awful Alzheimer's."

—&2—

South of Boston, Clare pulled off Interstate 95 onto the smaller
highway that ran over toward the Cape. She tried to count how
many exits there were to River Port, but she was used to riding
as Michael drove. They had come once a month or so in the early
years of their marriage. It had seemed to her even then that Michael felt it to be an obligation. There was never a rushing home
with the kind of enthusiasm she felt when the plane angled low
over Minneapolis and she began to imagine her father waiting for
them in the airport, began to imagine the oak tree by the back
deck at home and the way the early morning light would look in
her childhood bedroom the next day when she woke.

Michael's hometown, River Port, did not inspire enthusiasm. It sat on a hill overlooking the wide bay that cut in toward Rhode Island, and when she had heard it described that way she had imagined something charming: white cottages in sunlight over-looking glittering waters, sailboats, restaurants with umbrellas on the pier. Instead, it was an industrial city with streets that ran steeply toward a harbor of gray steel and rusty tankers. The water itself seemed oily, and the houses were mostly tenements that seemed to cling halfheartedly to the inclines. There were lopsided angles and ugly pastel vinyl siding and wrought iron knocked askew.

"It depresses the marrow of my bones," she had once told JoJo, and the two of them had tried many times to figure how Michael had emerged from such a place, how he had emerged from bleakness with such a gentle spirit and with such music at his fingertips. JoJo had said, "Maybe you should be grateful it's such an ugly place, because maybe that's why Michael had to create something beautiful for himself." After that, Clare imag-ined Michael as a boy, saw him leaning into the grade on Fourth Street, climbing with the sheet music for "Für Elise" tucked under his arm. She saw him at his lesson, sitting at the old upright piano in Mrs. Pinkney's spare bedroom, which smelled of mothballs, he had once told her. She saw his little-boy fingers finding the sharps and flats. It was what Clare always reminded herself whenever she came here. Out of darkness came the urge toward light.

She told herself that now, even as she reassured herself that she should have come. There was a house to be painted inside and out. There was a yard to be mowed, gardens to be tended. There was real work. Work she could do. And why shouldn't she?

Even as she coached herself onward, though, she was not at all sure. It was not that she feared Del's reaction. It was more that she feared seeing Michael's. Growing up in such a "circus" (his word, not hers) had made him protective of his family. From the time he was a kindergartner, he could remember people staring at his mothers dressed in purple and pink, at his fathers in their matching plaid golf pants. That attention had been one thing when his family was whole and prospering and content in their eccentricities. It was another thing entirely when Del and Belle had been unmoored from their faith in themselves, when their whole world was imploding inside poor Belle's brain. He was ashamed for their devastated pride. He wanted to shield them from all the attention they had called to themselves through the years, and which they couldn't deflect now, even though it was no longer welcome.

Clare knew this and also knew that he wanted to shield Belle and Del even from her. She knew this by a rough acknowledgment to herself. Michael had been more subtle about it. Last year, he had told her that he thought it was better if she didn't come up anymore with him to River Port. "It's too hard on you," he had said, and in parentheses behind his statement had been the implication, *given what you are going through yourself.* But she had understood it to mean that it was easier on him that way, not to see the judgment in her eyes when he agreed with Del that, yes, Belle was looking hale, and yes, she did carry on a conversation quite lucidly, and yes, he really did think that the new vitamin E therapy was working. Del believed that her sister was always on her way back to them. And Michael colluded with Del in this, even as he knew it was a lie. So, of course, it was easier for him if Clare didn't watch him in the midst of his consolatory deceit, his collusive denial. Maybe too it was easier for him if he didn't have to see his mother's true fate, see it loud and clear and terrible in his wife's unflinching eyes.

_⟨3⟨2_

Clare steered into the Klines' neighborhood, which was pleasant enough. It had always been a relief to her to get past the bleak views that distinguished River Port and back into this leafy neighborhood that might have been anywhere in suburban America. It was called Sea-to-Shining-Sea Estates and had been a new development when the Klines moved here in the sixties, but now the trees were mature and arched over the street.

Pulling up to the curb on Missouri Street, Clare stopped the Saturn in front of Del's house. Its clapboards were halfway scraped, and there was a ladder leaning just to one side of the bay window. It hurt Clare for Michael's sake, seeing the mirror houses this way. They looked like places where heartache made the floorboards creak at night, where lights burned at two in the morning. The yards were mowed but weedy at the edges. The perennial gardens that Del had tended in both yards were bedraggled. Rain and wind had beaten some of the taller spikes into submission. Foxgloves and delphiniums hung off bent stems, their petals flattened in the mud.

The doctors were now advising a nursing home for Belle. Michael had told Clare this much. But Del had brushed the idea off as cruelty, as the doctors prescribing too much by their training and not enough by their hearts. "It's not in me to do that," Del said, with an accusatory righteousness that Clare found both heartbreaking and maddening: As if it was *in* anyone to admit someone they loved to an institution. As if anyone *wanted* to do that.

Mommy Del had insisted to Michael that she could keep her twin at home. She would make the necessary adjustments, hire help. For one thing, she thought if they fixed up and sold one of the houses, it would help consolidate the burden. She decided it should be her own house: 128. "Wouldn't want to confuse Belle," she explained, which even Michael found absurd because the houses were so alike. Probably Michael thought, as Clare did, that

Mommy Belle was past noticing where she was and that Del, who wasn't, should have the comfort of her own home. But there was no dissuading Del. She wanted her own house scraped and painted and repaired up along the guttering. And she wanted Michael to do it.

Michael played the piano for a living. Mozart and Bach and Beethoven flowed out of him. Moods were set by the movement of his hands over a fine instrument, and yet he was always the only one who could fix the basement toilet in River Port or crawl up on the roof to replace some shingles or tear out the carpets where they had been ruined by the water fights that ensued whenever Belle needed a bath. They needed Michael so much, his two mothers, and all they could ask of him was his manual labor. They didn't have the words for what they really needed of him.

And he knew this. He was their son. He always went to them. One two three four. He went on his day off, up and back in one day, coming home to drop exhausted into bed. He went on holidays. While Clare had been in Los Angeles, he had gone every week, and now here he was, away from his wife, spending his vacation scraping Del's house. He was guilty about that, true; they had so little time together, but . . . one two three four.

Clare swung the car door open, stood, and at the same moment spotted Michael coming through the side yard, drinking iced tea and wiping his brow. His eyebrows were pulled together into a sharp brooding **V**, a look that seemed incongruous with the torn jeans and the baseball cap. His gaze shifted to the street, and instantly his stride snagged on the realization that, yes, that was his wife parked there. The realization passed over his face like a shadow thrown from a cloud.

It would have been impossible for her to miss the look, though he forced an eagerness into his step and light into his smile. He came toward her quickly. Her hand was on the bouquet she had brought, and she stared at it a moment, gathering herself, swallowing back the pain she felt: He did not want her here.

"Clare," he said. "Is everything okay?"

"Yes," she answered, in a voice that was too high because she was forcing buoyancy into it. It sounded to her as though she had inhaled helium. But he didn't seem to notice.

"What are you doing here?" Already, she thought, he was wondering how he could hurry her away, or failing that, how he could juggle her with Belle and Del inside the other house, the one past delusions and the one dependent upon them.

"Brought you these," Clare said, holding out the flowers. She smiled into his eyes.

He tilted his head to one side, as though she were an abstract painting in an art museum that eluded him. If he could only look at it from another angle, he would understand. What was she doing in River Port?

She stretched the bouquet toward him. Each blossom had been nurtured by her. She had smuggled the hollyhock into the country as ripe seeds, pilfered into her palm at Monet's garden at Giverny. She had carefully chosen the chartreuse tobacco and old Italian-heritage sweet peas of a distinctive purple and had fretted through the years over the tending of her Fortune Teller roses. And today they were all she had to give her husband. All she had to give that he might comfortably accept.

"What are you doing here?" he pressed.

"I delivered," she said.

"You drove all the way up here to bring me flowers?"

She nodded.

"Why?"

"Because I love you."

His smile twitched at the corners. He was staring at the flowers. She thought it was easier for him than looking at her. He no doubt felt himself a traitor, felt the panicked betrayal beating in his chest.

He didn't want to hurt her; she knew that with certainty. It was the last thing he would want. He didn't want to hurt her anymore than he wanted to risk hurting Belle and Del with her presence. "Thank you," he said finally. "C'mon in, and we'll hunt up a vase." He was trying so hard, fighting himself for her sake.

"Can't stay," she said, for his.

His eyes went to hers. "Why not?"

"Because I love you."

The sun had gone behind the fringe of pines on the road just before she turned off Route One. It still hung in the highest branches of the tallest trees, making them look like brushes that had been dipped in bronze. Now, in the stretching shade, every color took on blue. The ocean, when she saw it between the trees, was so blue it was black.

The road narrowed going down the peninsula. She passed the Churchhouse farmstand. Strawberries were in season, a deep red in their green baskets. PEAS! a sign proclaimed. The summer was slower coming on here. It would be short and intense, she knew: a quick burgeoning of green followed by setting fruit. Just before the frost, the watermelon would come with the pumpkins.

Her impulse was to stop and touch the vegetables—the cool husk of the peas, the ruffled heft of the lettuce—and hear the barnyard dog snore under the table and smell the fresh-cut hay, to leave with something that had been rooted in the earth that morning, growing moist cell by cell, sweetening on the soil and sun and rain.

But she didn't stop. She was hungry for more than strawberries on the stem, and she was yearning for the Biscuit, hoping it would still be in business on the Sky Hill wharf. She was hoping that she could sit in one of the booths by the window and watch the lights of the harbor boats winking on the waves. The last ferry would arrive from the island in another hour or so, and the gray boards of the dock would fill with people waiting for it, and then the vacationers would wave in the green light of the wharf lamps and their voices would come like bird cries off the water, and they would carry their bright backpacks and L. L. Bean bags down the ramp and toward the lot, where the headlights would come on and swing across the waterfront and climb up the hill through the trees, leaving town, leaving Sky Hill to the waves lapping and the night insects sawing and the boats shifting *thunk, thunk, thunk* against their solid moorings.

Sky Hill had stayed in her memory like a scene in one of those snow globes that tourists bring back from trips. The Eiffel Tower caught in water and fake snow. Or the Statue of Liberty. That's how the weathered village on the peninsula and the island miles beyond it in the ocean, that's how they both seemed to her: swimming in her memory, magnified by it.

How much of that was because of Riley? Because of what had happened here? He had followed her home that first day he pushed her into the ocean inlet. She was dripping with salt water. It stung her eyes, made them red. But she was too mad to cry. She pedaled her bicycle like a piston, furious. He had kept the bumper of his truck just behind her. It felt like a beast of prey. He felt like a beast.

Tearing down the Prentiss drive, she had headed for her aunt and uncle and their bolstering indignation. But the threat of this did not deter Riley. He followed her right into the circle drive at the gardener's cottage. He got out and followed her to the rock patio out back where her aunt was setting out supper on the picnic table.

"What happened to you?" Fran had asked, pausing as she set down the stack of plates.

"He happened to me," Clare said, whirling to point at her lanky assailant, who was smirking.

Fran started to laugh. "That didn't take long," she said.

Clare felt stung, undefended.

"What's her name?" Riley asked Fran, nodding at Clare.

"That's my niece Clare," she said. "What have you done to her?"

He shrugged. "She said she loved the water."

"Who's he?" Clare asked her aunt.

"Oh, that's Riley Brackett. You better be nice to him, or you won't get any lobster this summer."

"Why? Is he in charge of seafood in the whole Atlantic Ocean?"

Riley laughed, and Fran said, "To repeat, Riley, this is Clare. Clare, this is Riley. I'm going back in to get the muffins out of the oven. You'll have to speak to one another now." And she had disappeared.

Riley looked at Clare then and chorused, "You said you loved the water." He had a crooked grin, and he was gazing up at her from under downcast lashes. He seemed contrite.

She should've known better. Instead, she started to laugh. "I like *looking* at it."

"Oh, no," he said. "You're not one of those, are you?"

"One of what?"

"One of those girls who uses her head to do what the rest of her's more suited for? You've got skin, don't you? Use it."

"What's that supposed to mean?"

"It means you can look at an ocean and say, oh what a pretty color blue. Like it was something that would look nice painted on a plate, real swirly. Or you can get out there—all of you. You can get *in* it. There's a reason God made you so you wouldn't melt in water." He paused a minute, then added, "Like a sugar cube."

Clare had grinned then in spite of herself and had felt the flirtation bloom in her like sand kicked up from the bottom of the ocean. It obscured her own good sense, and she knew it. But she looked up from under her own lashes and was saved from making an answer when Fran showed up with the muffins. Her aunt asked Riley to ring the dinner chime for Tig, and then Tig showed up and thwacked Riley on the back affectionately, and Riley sat down at the table as though he belonged, and soon it was dark and the fireflies were out and the mosquitoes were biting, and sometime after that supper was over and it was bedtime: all too soon.

But night was never long in Maine, not in the summer anyway. Clare had woken early that next morning, just after five o'clock, when she heard Tig close the screen door behind him, and the first thing she thought of was not the fact that her mother was dying. Instead, Clare thought of Riley. She thought of the dimple in his chin, the kind someone had once told her was imprinted when the devil got ahold of you so he could hold you still while he took a long meaningful look in your eyes. Could be true; Riley was puckish. And he had curly hair. She lay there in bed with her gable window bright as stained glass—the first sun through the clean green leaves and the blue beyond, the Maine blue—and she wondered what it would be like to touch his hair, to take a coil of it in her fingers and stretch it out out out, let it snap back. Just wondering made her grin.

—⟨⟩⟨⟩—

Looking ahead, Clare saw the steeple, its finial bright as it reached up to pierce the last light of the sun. And then she was around the big curve and coming down the hill into the town itself: Sky Hill with its window boxes frothing over on houses weathered gray and its painted crustaceans clawing at the sky—FRESH LOBSTERS 4 SALE—and the old wooden traps piled in picturesque heaps by the waterfront. The weeds would grow on up through those traps, Clare knew, and they would bloom. They would be goldenrod.

She parked in the Hilltop Inn's lot and hoped for a room. There was no one at the desk, though she could smell food in the dining room. She walked toward the clatter of the evening meal, and finally she caught the hostess's eye. "Table for one?" the young woman asked.

"I was hoping for a room for one," Clare said.

"Are you a Leo?" the hostess asked.

Clare squeezed her eyebrows together, trying to follow. She felt as she did in France sometimes, right off the transatlantic flight. It took a while, through her exhaustion, for spoken French to sort itself into syllables she could command—hearing or speaking. Now her puzzlement must have shown, because the hostess laughed amiably and said, "It's just that you must've been born under a lucky star. Someone decided to spend another night on the island. Gave up their room."

Clare laughed. "I could use a lucky star."

She got settled in the room, which overlooked the garden and not the water, and then she went back out into the dusk. The ocean was fresh on her face, and though it was July, she pulled her sweater closed and buttoned it. She made for the neon light of the Biscuit.

The restaurant was just the way she remembered it. Nets draped from the ceiling, and in them were suspended shells, gargantuan lobster claws that looked petrified, and also starfish. Candles burned on the tables inside little lanterns, and outside on the deck overhanging the water, several groups of people huddled together around the picnic tables. They sat hunched in their windbreakers, with beach towels draped over their legs. They shivered when they drank from their dark bottles of beer, but they looked as happy as anyone Clare had seen in months. They looked like people who had been kept in cities or colleges or jobs for too many months straight, trapped in their own concerns—the mortgage, the fluctuations of their GPAs, the boss's subtext, the results of that blood test—and now they were released, threaded up on the strings of leisure and airlifted beyond their lives. They looked the way she felt: free.

Was the solace in the air? Or in the beer? Or just in the cool dew on the bottle of beer that you wiped on the leg of your shorts? Was it the salt on the fried clams? Or the minced pickle in the tartar sauce? Was it the last pink of the sun going down, caught in that western cloud behind them? What was here in Sky Hill that could free those people from themselves, free Clare from herself? And why couldn't she pack it like lobsters in seaweed or hoard it as she had once hoarded bags of Maine's special Humpty Dumpty Salt & Vinegar potato chips? Why couldn't she press it away in a book, like the daisies Riley had picked on her last trip to the island? Why couldn't she pack a little of it, drop some off for Michael in River Port?

The waitress came, and Clare ordered from memory without glancing at the menu for anything more than the nostalgia of seeing its hand-drawn shells and lobsters and ears of corn. She ordered the steamed artichoke and the scallop chowder, large not small, please.

Ah, the Biscuit, where coastal Maine met the Upper East Side. Decades earlier, Suzy Easton, a local lobsterman's daughter, had caught the eye of Alex Morton, of old money and a summer estate on Meguntic Cove. They had married, and he had brought his trust fund and his travel-informed flare for cooking to the Salty Biscuit on the wharf.

When it came, the chowder tasted just as Clare remembered it. Tarragon was the secret, she thought now. Her palate had been less developed the last time she ate here, but now she was pretty sure. Fresh tarragon and onions cooked in butter with celery seed. She would try to make it at home sometime, although it would be missing the main ingredient. It would be missing Sky Hill.

She was taking her last bite of the chowder, wiping it up with the shallot-and-sage biscuits that made the place famous, when her cell phone throbbed against her leg. She jumped in surprise. She had been far out the window with her eyes and her memory, watching the purple line of the land meld into the black water and the sky sink down into them. Now she suddenly saw only herself reflected back in the window: Clare McClendon. Back to reality.

"Hello," she whispered, embarrassed to be heard doing something so citified and despicable here in the old Biscuit, here within earshot of the same, steady waves.

"Clare?" Michael said. "Where are you?"

All she could do was laugh.

The next morning, Clare pulled on a denim jacket and crept through the sleeping hotel and out the door. The air was full of the ocean and still pink with the sunrise. It seemed to have a crystalline depth that magnified like water. Each shingle was distinct on the roof of the landing's fish house, each pebble on the boat launch, each curl of water that laid itself up on the shore, then fell back.

It was so early that the bicycle rental place was still locked up, so Clare walked past it and kept going, heading down the last long prong of the promontory. She hardly felt her feet on the pavement. She was flying with the gulls. She was the sun on shiny leaves, the spice of evergreens, the sensation of salt. She was the planet Venus hanging up there.

That was something she had learned because of that summer: how the morning star was also the evening star, sometimes the planet Venus, and how if you knew how to look for it, you could see it there all day, still shining white. Before sunrise today, she had crawled out of bed, beckoned by the planet's brightness, glinting there in the deep suede blue of dawn. She had stood at the window of her room until the sun had flamed up red. Clare had measured then how far apart they were, Venus from the sun. All day, they would keep their distance—the breadth of her hand. All day, she would know where in the sky to look for the daylight star.

Pausing at the rock bridge that spanned the inlet, she looked out across the sheet of water: the Atlantic. It was calm as a pond this morning, that great expanse. There were boats, their sails caught broadside by the horizontal sun, filled with the early light as much as with the faint breeze. They seemed hardly to move.

Clare had read Melville since she had been here last, and she had been struck by his observation that "reflection and water will always be wedded." It was reflection, what happened to her here, so much more than it was thought. As she could see the mirror image of herself cast back at her from the surface of the deep green pool under the bridge, so too there was something of her inner life cast back at her from the ocean itself. She was surprised at how serene it was, this reflection of herself, how suddenly serene.

The road rose again on the other side of the bridge. There was an underwater ledge that connected this last bit to the mainland, to the continent itself. But water overcame it except on the lowest of spring tides. The point was really an island, and Last Look lay at its farthest tip, the sea a sheen around it. It always had seemed to Clare to be suspended in light.

At the open gate to the estate, she hesitated. Nearly two decades had passed since she had seen the Prentisses. But Aunt Fran, living back in Minneapolis near her family since Tig's death, received a Christmas card every year, and without fail there were regards sent along to Clare. In recent years, they had seen her on the news, Mrs. Prentiss wrote, "and weren't we thrilled." Eventually, there had been news of Mr. Prentiss's death.

Curiosity won out. Old affection, too. Clare crossed onto the property. The crushed shells of the driveway gave like sand under her feet, and she was aware of the noise, of how it must herald her approach in the parklike quiet of the grounds. She could see a gardener off by the vegetable garden, and she twinged for Tig. He had loved these acres, had plunged into them up to his elbows. He had died here before the volunteer rescue crew could get the ambulance out from town. Aunt Fran had said at the wake in Minneapolis that he would not have wanted to die anyplace else. He had loved Last Look as though it had been his own. He had tended it with that kind of care.

As Clare rounded a last bend in the drive, she could see that Mrs. Prentiss was on the porch. "Who's that sneaking up on us?" the elderly woman called, rising from the swing and coming to stand by the stairs, her hand on a column, steadying herself. Her hair was as lavender as her sweater now, Clare thought, and it just might be the same sweater. Clare had hardly ever seen her out of that unraveling sweater, and that kind of loyalty had appealed to Clare even as a teenager.

"It's Clare McClendon," she called. "Sorry to be so surreptitious, but I started out on a walk and just kept coming. Like a homing pigeon."

"Oh, my dear, I'm so glad," Mrs. Prentiss said, holding out her hand.

Clare climbed the steps and grasped Mrs. Prentiss's hand. Time seemed to have worked away at Mrs. Prentiss, worked away at her as waves mull over bits of broken glass, rubbing them past shininess into soft opacity. Mrs. Prentiss was worn to velvet. "Come sit with me and have some tea. You know I've lost my Howard," she said. "Two years ago this coming September."

"I was so sorry to hear it," Clare told her, as she settled into the cushions of a wicker chair. A reflected net of sun on water shimmered above them, moving across the porch ceiling. Steam rose from a porcelain teapot painted with sweet peas; the steam seemed like a rising veil of sunshine. Mrs. Prentiss poured her guest a careful cup, then a second for herself. Clare noticed a palsy in her hands.

"So now I'm here only by the good graces of the children," Mrs. Prentiss said, then added in a winklike whisper, "who all sleep late."

Clare laughed softly.

"I'm so glad you've come to see our Riley."

"Oh, no," Clare stammered, "not really. I had some time off after the trial . . ."

"I watched your channel just to see your reports. I was so worried about whether you were getting enough rest, working those hours like that. Good heavens. But wasn't that awful that the jury let him go?" Mrs. Prentiss exhaled, referring to the accused movie star. "Charisma buys justice in this world, don't think it doesn't. Those baby blues of his." She settled back with her cup clasped in both hands. "So they gave you a little breather after the verdict?"

"Yes, and I was at a loss for what to do with myself, and I started driving north, just playing really, and here I am. First time since I was seventeen."

Mrs. Prentiss leaned forward and laid her hand on Clare's knee. "Oh, dear, you must go see him. It's all in the world he needs. Didn't you get something from Laurie? His little wife, a darling girl. I ran into her up in town—she's working three jobs, they say—and I told her I'd seen him myself and knew all about it and, for heaven's sake, get ahold of Clare. She'd be happy to help, I told her. Clare's a good girl, don't you know?"

Clare laughed uncomfortably.

"She said she had no idea how to find you, and I said, not to worry, that your Aunt Fran kept me posted. I happened to know that you were living in that little town on the Hudson. Howard and I had friends who lived there years ago, in a house on a hill, yellow. Do you know it?"

Clare tried to think, but her mind was spun far away from the Hudson River valley. She couldn't place the house.

"Beautiful home, a turret facing to the east, as I remember. Anyway, I ran into Laurie right in Herb's store on the wharf. So I picked up the pay phone and had your number and address in no time. I handed the receiver to her, and she dropped it like it was hot. She said she couldn't barge in on you, couldn't bother you. I told her that was nonsense, but she wouldn't budge. The best I could get her to do was drop you a line. Lucky that Herb still rents that corner of his store to the post office. Every year, they try to propose a move to a bigger building, and every year, it gets slapped down. We don't like to change here." She paused, as if to reorient herself. "Anyway, I told her not to stand on ceremony at a time like this, just drop you a postcard."

Clare nodded, for lack of any other response.

Mrs. Prentiss said in a hushed voice: "She was a bit backward even about that. But I insisted. And I thought she did a fine job. It was my idea to tell you about the children, so she squeezed that in there. Riley had those two girls out here to see me last summer, one on each shoulder, and Clare, I tell you, it's like him all over again, two little shadows of Riley. How in this world will we all survive that?"

She laughed and breathed in a sip of tea and looked out at the brilliance spread across the surface of the water. "Yes," she continued. "You have to see Riley. Bless his good heart. It's all in the world he needs."

The Bracketts' house was not by the water. Lobstermen couldn't afford to live by the water anymore, the waiter at the Biscuit had told Clare the night before. Most of the homes in the village had sold in recent years to CFAs, people who Come From Away. They bought the homes along the harbor and tidied up the landscaping, kept everything painted fresh. The men who owned the rough-and-ready working boats lived back in the woods and drove in at five in the morning most days, rowed out to their moored boats, and thrummed off into the rising sun to haul.

Clare remembered how much money Riley had made, even working as a sternman on his father's and uncle's boats. He had been nothing but a kid, but he had taken a percentage of each day's haul, an impressive percentage, Clare had thought at the time. With that and the tips he made delivering lobsters to the summer people, who invariably doted on him, he had made great money. That summer, he had saved enough to buy an old but sturdy twenty-eight-footer. Wouldn't happen now, based on what the waiter said. According to him, it took two hundred thousand just to break into the business. The young man spoke with authority on the subject, but Clare observed to herself that he had a distinctly New York accent himself. He was a CFA, and a naive one at that. He still thought he could sympathize enough with the locals to be accepted as one. He still thought he could love Sky Hill enough to belong to it.

Though she was resigned to her mission, it took Clare a while to find Riley's place. Mrs. Prentiss had had no idea where it was, and when Clare had asked directions in Herb Cote's store on the wharf, a salesclerk had told her it was out on Folsom's road. She had bought the detailed Maine atlas for reference and had then sat in the car for half an hour, eating Humpty Dumpty chips and grazing a fingernail along the map of the Sky Hill peninsula. There didn't seem to be a Folsom's road anywhere on it. The chip bag was empty before she remembered that natives had a way of giving directions based on the names of families who lived—or had once lived, six generations back—on a point or a corner or a road.

She drove in the direction that the salesclerk had gestured toward, and when nothing caught her eye, not on a mailbox or anything else, she humbled herself and asked directions from a woman who was pulling weeds from her bed of cosmos. "That'd be up here to Yorks with the satellite dish, then you go up the hill twice and then down the road by the tractor," the woman said, turning back to her work without a single other word. That was another thing Clare had forgotten. Her uncle had told her that a real Mainer, if asked for directions by a tourist, would say,

"You can't get there from here." She thought these directions might be of the same species: There wasn't a single right or left in there. And weren't tractors movable objects?

Anyway, Clare followed the instructions. At the satellite dish, there was only one way to turn that ran uphill. She drove up it, dipped into a shallow valley, then climbed again before coming around a curve and down, where she saw a tractor sunk to its axle in mud. It was rusted in place. There were lupines going to seed all the way around it and white morning glories twining up its frame. Clearly, it had been there long enough to become a landmark.

At the end of this spur road, which was unpaved and still rutted from mud season, she came to a house. It was nothing but a crooked little cape turned gray by the wind and salt off the ocean, which was nowhere in sight though she could still smell it. A gleaming boat was set up on a frame in the side yard, and it was bigger than the house itself and certainly in finer shape. In black letters, its name was painted on the bow: *The Eclipse*. The meaning ran through her like a current of electricity.

Dogs barked out back, but no animal came glowering around front to threaten her. So she got out of the car and walked up the wooden steps to the door, knocked, and waited. A raggedy pot of pansies bloomed by the door. No one had deadheaded them in a while, and they were about to play out from the heat and from the effort of making seed. She couldn't help herself. She bent and snapped off the spent blooms, the swollen seed pods. She gave them a second chance at thriving.

When she looked up, a girl of about five was standing with her face pressed against the screen, her nose flattened across her face. "Hi," said the child, squeezing the greeting out of her smooshed lips.

"Hi, there," Clare said. "Is your mother here?"

"Mum!" yelled the child, rearing back from the screen, but

keeping both palms pressed against it, her fingers splayed. "Clare Mac is here."

Nobody had called her Clare Mac since she was seventeen. Nobody had called her that since Riley had reached to hold her that last night, reached to haul her back into his grasp that last time, trying to save her. Now, reflexively, she touched her hair, as though it was giving her away. How could this child know who she was? Occasionally, someone recognized her on the street and pointed out her own identity to her: "Hey, you're Clare Mc-Clendon." As if she didn't know. But it didn't happen often—and then mainly in New York, where there was such a high concentration of news addicts. Fortunately, she was one of those broadcasters who had a screen personality that completely transformed her everyday appearance. A certain poise defined her to the camera. But she didn't travel with that poise ever. Certainly not today.

"How do you know I'm Clare Mac?" she said, kneeling to look at the child face-to-face.

The little girl said, "I'm Mandy." Then, she hollered again, "Mum!"

No answer came from the depths of the house.

"Maybe she's out in the garden," Clare suggested.

"She's asleep."

"Asleep?" Clare checked her watch. It was now eleven o'clock in the morning, and she was used to being a late sleeper compared to Mainers. She hadn't considered . . .

"My sister was puking," Mandy said.

"Oh," Clare said.

"Mum!" Mandy bellowed again.

"Maybe you should go get her."

"Okay." The girl turned and disappeared into the dark rooms of the house where Clare's sight couldn't follow. She felt sneaky even trying. So she turned around and looked up the road by which she had come and by which she now longed to leave. This wasn't what she had expected. Sad, she had expected. Sad, she could understand. What had happened was terribly sad. This was sad and stinted.

"You came," a woman said through the screen. The words were blunt, uninflected. They conveyed no surprise or pleasure or gratitude.

Clare jumped and clutched at the collar of her cotton dress. "You scared me," she said. "You must be Laurie." The woman's face was as expressionless as her opening words. She was shorter than Clare and full around her hips, a mother. Her eyes were dark and alert, though they were smudged underneath with exhaustion. Her skin had a gray undertone, though it looked roughed-up red, raw.

Clare waited to be let in. She had been invited to come, after all. But instead, Laurie Brackett said, "Just a minute." She left with her bare feet splatting against the bare floorboards and returned in a pair of those Velcro sports sandals that Clare saw people wearing even in airports now: Third World chic. Worn loose, they seemed to detonate with each step Laurie took toward Clare.

Laurie came out on the porch and then stepped down off it, waited for Clare to follow. Little Mandy came out, slamming the door behind her. "You stay here," Laurie scolded her. "In case Jessie wakes up."

"No," Mandy wailed.

"Hush yourself up," Laurie said and started walking around the house, down toward what looked to be an orchard. Clare guessed she was supposed to follow. She made a sympathetic face to Mandy, who turned away from her. In the sunlight, Clare could see how much the child's hair was like Riley's, curly and almost scarlet, threaded through with copper. She had always thought his hair was wasted on a boy. And she was right: It looked beautiful on his little daughter.

"You could've called," Laurie said over her shoulder. Her blond hair bounced in a ponytail that seemed pert and youthful, belying the lines on her face that were made deeper and more obvious by the glaring midday sun.

"I'm sorry." Clare felt stung. Had she misinterpreted the woman's request for help? Hadn't Laurie asked her to come? Hadn't Mrs. Prentiss insisted? "I thought..."

"You just thought you'd come make nice."

"I thought you wanted to speak with me. I thought you wanted my help in some way."

"I do want your help," Laurie said. "But I'd just as soon not have to look at you."

"Oh," Clare said, the word coming out like the grunt that follows being punched in the stomach.

The two of them were standing in a maze of trees. The sun was high, slicing down toward Clare in a way that made it difficult to lift her gaze. She wasn't sure if it was the sun making her feel dizzy or the turn of the conversation. She wished she could find Venus, just to steady herself.

Laurie Brackett sighed, squinting off into the distance. "I'm sorry," she said. "It's not your fault. Last night was a bad one. Since the accident, I've taken a job at a shoe factory in Bangor."

"Isn't that an hour away?" Clare asked, trying to remember, but also trying to keep the tone of the conversation cordial.

"An hour-twenty. Plus I work the eleven to seven: graveyard. When I got home this morning and picked up the girls from their grammy, the little one was tossing up her socks. Dry heaves by the time I got to her. She hasn't been the same since she lost her daddy. Any little thing hits her tummy wrong." Laurie shook her head. "And Mandy's all vinegar. Mad at me as much as she's mad at losing him."

"She seems bright."

Laurie turned and gave Clare such a direct look that it might have made a slapping sound on contact. "Takes after her daddy."

Clare felt the accusation. She groped for words, but only thought to ask, "How did she know who I was?"

Laurie laughed, but it was not pleasant to hear. "Clare Mac," she said. "We've all lived with you for years."

"What's that supposed to mean?"

"It means that your name has been on Riley Brackett's tongue ever since I've been involved with him. When he tells the girls a bedtime story, the superwoman is always named Clare Mac, and when he lets them go through his old pictures, there is Clare Mac, Clare Mac, Clare Mac. Mandy has one of the cards you gave him hanging on her wall. You're famous to my girls. You're the mummy they should've had. Riley made no bones about it."

"He was wrong to do that," Clare said, distancing herself from Riley even as his wife's words sunk down into her, were absorbed into actual realization. She had had no inkling of this, though it made her feel guilty to hear it. It made her feel several layers of guilt: Seventeen years ago, she had walked away and kept the memory of Riley as she had kept the memory of the lunar eclipse they had watched together, something rare and gone. She hadn't dwelled on his memory, had rarely done more than idly wonder what might have become of him, and meanwhile he was building shrines to her in the home he had made with another woman. Learning this made her feel even mildly traitorous for loving her husband so much. For having found happiness when Riley hadn't. When Laurie hadn't.

"He was wrong to do most things he ever did," Laurie said. "But he was their daddy. And they loved him." She paused, looked hard at the grass around the roots of a particularly gnarled tree. "Who am I kidding? I loved him too, despite the foolishness, 'cause that was all from his heart. I could see that. Of course, I could see that." She looked squarely at Clare and said, "I did love him."

"You talk like he's dead," Clare said.

Laurie swung her eyes back to the ground. "He is to me," she said. There was a sudden solemnity in her tone.

They both heard Mandy's voice from the top of the hill and turned together to see her leading her sister by the hand. The little one was still in her diaper, picking up each bare foot high enough to step over the tall blades of grass. She was a little blonde.

"Won't be long," Laurie said with black resignation, "till he'll be dead to them too."

Standing on the top deck of a ferry called the Nora B., *Clare* watched Captain Harris Barnicle lean from the pilothouse and tell the college boy on shore to toss up the lines. The boy, unmistakably a CFA, was knobby-kneed in his Nike hikers and skinny and tanned, a stretch version of the type who had always helped out with the ferries that ran between Sky Hill and Ledgemere Island. This one had the usual look of proud purpose on his face, as well as the usual cultivated nonchalance, trying to appear as though he thought no one was watching but hoping everyone was. No doubt his name was different from that of the last kid she'd seen throw in the line, but Clare would've recognized him anywhere. He was having the time of his life.

"Going to church at Sky Hill," Riley had called it, sneering about the CFAs who waitressed in the Biscuit and hauled in lines on the ferry and mopped the floors at Herb's store: They were all so wide-eyed and effusive about the place. They would get up at dawn, not to fish or haul traps or shell scallops but just to hike out to Widow's Ladder and watch the sun bulge up out of the Atlantic. But Clare had told Riley that he didn't know Sky Hill himself because he had never known anyplace else. "What kind of double-loop knot is that to say?" he had asked. But she could tell by the way he looked at her that it was the kind of double-loop knot that made him crazy for her.

As long as the ferry was still in the harbor, among the anchored yachts and sailboats, Clare stood with her bag at her feet. But when it broke into open water, she sat down at the stern and shielded her eyes with the flat of one hand. There were lobster boats out here, cutting curved swaths through the choppy sea, letting down their traps as the seagulls swarmed them like tossed confetti. The boats' colorful markers bobbed behind them like water tops, marking their spots. Riley had tried to teach her how to read the markers. They were a hieroglyphic language understood by the men and women who made their livings in the coastal waters: Someone had yellow and white, another had blue and red, yet another teal and pink. She wondered what colors belonged to Riley these days.

Scanning her eyes across all the bobbing buoys, nothing struck her with meaning. She couldn't read them anymore. But when she leaned her head back against the netting strung from the boat's railings and cocked her head to the sun and closed her eyes and opened herself, she understood where she was. She deciphered it through every pore. This moment had not changed from the last she had experienced like it. One moment echoed the other.

Even Captain Barnicle looked the same, a solid surefooted man in sensible shoes and khaki clothes. He wore his same captain's hat, and the same white beard encircled his red face, framing his open smile. He shaved his upper lip so there was no moustache to hide behind: He had nothing to hide. Seeing her coming up the plank this morning, he had greeted Clare warmly and had remembered her name. She thought he must have one of those eighteen-inch satellite dishes on the side of his shingled cape, and during the winter, when the *Nora B.* forged only three mail runs a week to Ledgemere, he must turn the television on and watch satellite broadcasts as the dim afternoons sank into the long dark nights. He must have seen her covering the trial, though he made no mention of it, just shouldered her bag himself and led her to the best spot on deck to make the crossing. "Settle yourself in," he had told her.

Settle in she had. And now she heard Captain Barnicle talking to his passengers, and it might have been all those years before, when she had taken the ferry out to Ledgemere. Then, too, the captain had stopped the boat in the narrow channel that ran between the nearest islands, where the family of artists had made their homes. The Winslows had been painting for three generations on the islands off Sky Hill. Their weather-gray homes were scattered across the swells of land. Their graves were marked by stark white crosses in the barren windswept cemetery on the highest rise there. And their stories, the stories of their lives, were proudly repeated up and down the coast of Maine. It was the same now as last time.

Only Clare had changed. She knew things she hadn't known before, and these facts floated through her consciousness like detritus of the life she had since lived, detritus borne on the floods of nostalgia. Nora Barnacle was James Joyce's wife, for one thing. Clare had read *Ulysses* and parts of *Finnegans Wake* and also a biography of Nora. Certainly this ferry was named after Captain Harris's wife, a brittle woman with blazing red cheeks, as Clare remembered. But there was that literary connection too, that other Nora B., whether it was intentional on the captain's part or not.

These men of the sea marked their lives in seasons. There were some who carved driftwood in the winter, others who painted birds. Riley had once introduced her to a giant fisherman, whose shadow had covered both of them as they stood talking. He knitted in the winter, Riley told her later. Every woman on the peninsula wanted one of his sweaters. So, who knew, maybe Captain Harris Barnicle didn't watch television. Maybe he read Irish literature in the dark season.

And the Winslows, she knew more about them as well. She had loved their art when she was seventeen and had seen it in the galleries on Ledgemere. Their paintings were rendered realistically. Looking at them, she could almost smell the sea. With the money she had earned at the library, she had bought a print, and she had wept when Riley brought it to her, signed by Sam Winslow and framed. "He's nothing but an old salt," Riley had said, as embarrassed by her tears as he was pleased by them. Since then, Clare had read the art critics' stance on the Winslows and had second-guessed her own teenage sensibility (though she did still keep the Winslow hanging in her bedroom, and something in her did still love it or loved what it had meant to her, loved how it had stirred her).

Yes, she knew about the other Nora Barnacle and how the *New Yorker*'s critic had to hold his nose to look at a Winslow. She knew a lot she hadn't known the last time she took a sun-soak on the way over to Ledgemere. The sun caused cancer, wasn't that another?

Count the things that haven't changed, she urged herself, recoiling. Count the unchangeables: the rush of the wind, the taste of the salt if she licked her lips, how she could see the gulls open their mouths but could hear their harsh cries only in her imagination because they were drowned out by the sound of the big engine rumbling somewhere below her. Some things hadn't changed. Some things were just the same. Imagine what it must be like for Riley. Everything was the same as it had been when they were seventeen years old. No wife named Laurie. No little girls, one with red hair, the other with blond. No memory that Clare had ever gone away.

The doctor had said it was an amnesia psychosis brought on by the accident. A severe head injury. He was perfectly correct, the doctor, as he told Clare the medical diagnosis, but he looked so little like a professional that she found it hard to process his words. He was a young man, probably no older than she, and he was fat. His skin glistened pinkly in a way she found grotesque. She thought it was vaguely like the surface of an exposed liver.

Clare had insisted on seeing Riley's doctor before she would consider seeing Riley himself. And Laurie had relented and had made the call to arrange it. Clare had gone to the doctor's office, which was in his home and overlooked the water. There were binoculars on his windowsill, and she thought he was probably from old money and had moved here to lead a respectable life, a quiet one. She thought he must like nothing more than to watch the birds. She speculated that he must barely have made it through medical school. He must have passed the medical boards solely on his family's expectation that he would. She always did this, she thought as she sat there. When she was disconcerted, she made up unflattering stories about whoever was in her line of sight. She manufactured the facts of their lives to assuage herself.

"It's reversible, right?" she had asked him. "Riley's amnesia?"

He had shrugged his bulbous shoulders. "That depends," he said.

"On what?"

"Well, that's where the medical books can't help us. I might as well be one of those medieval practitioners who set their poor sick patients out on the road, in the hope that some passerby might have seen the affliction before and might be able to tell them how to cure it." He had gone on to tell her that a condition like Riley's sometimes occurred in alcoholics. Their remote memory survived the deficiencies of their liquid diet, but their short-term recall did not. Their recent lives seemed lopped off and cast away, like an amputated leg. They were left only with what had once happened to them.

"In alcoholics," he said, "we can at least treat it by replacing what they're not getting from drinking every meal. We can get at the memory loss through nutrition and with thiamine infusions. But with head trauma, it's more complicated. Riley's memory could spontaneously come back next week or next year. But if this hangs on for two years, we can pretty much figure it's going to be a permanent condition."

"Permanent?"

"Afraid so."

"Then where do I fit into all this? If there's nothing you can do..." Clare said, suddenly wishing she didn't fit into all this. "I haven't even seen him for seventeen years."

"You're an experiment," the fat doctor had told her, rubbing both of his palms idly over the stretched fabric of his shirt. He looked like a pregnant woman caressing her unborn child.

"An experiment?" Clare snorted.

"He seems to be fixated on you."

"Why me?"

"You were in an accident with him?"

"Yes, but that was years and years and years ago."

"Well, apparently, when he woke up from this accident, it was as if he was waking up from that one years and years and years ago, as you say."

Clare was struck silent.

"And he's been frantic about you ever since."

"Hasn't someone told him the truth? Hasn't anyone told him that I'm okay, and in fact I'm thirty-four years old now and married to someone else?"

"Of course we've told him. But he can't capture the truth. It seems to elude him."

"Then what difference will it make for him to see me?"

The doctor looked sheepish. "His wife was hoping you had aged badly."

Clare rolled her eyes. "That's sophomoric." She caught herself. "I'm sorry," she said. "It just seems so outlandish, all of it. There must be some medical technique. Or some psychiatric approach..."

"Of course, you'd feel that way. But you must take into account certain variables. Riley Brackett is a strong man who has moved himself out to the island and is living there as though he were a boy with his whole life ahead of him. He will not acknowledge his wife or their two daughters, whom I must tell you, he doted on. He loved them very much. He was a famous dad around here."

She smiled.

The doctor went on: "Riley Brackett has always been very beloved. And he's always done exactly what he wanted to do. You must know that."

She nodded. Of course she knew that.

"Now, he's handling this the way he wants to handle this. And everyone is letting him."

"Wants to...?" she asked. "You're implying that he has a choice."

"Well," said the fat doctor as he patted his own big belly, "there is the possibility of confabulation."

"You mean he's making it up?"

"No, not at all. He's had a serious blow, and he's lost part of his life. It's gone. But I won't dismiss the possibility that he's compensating for the resulting confusion by substituting missing facts with fantasy."

"Fantasy?"

The doctor cleared his throat. "I understand he hadn't exactly gotten over your love affair."

"It was hardly an affair," she said testily. "We were not much more than children."

"In any case, he had never gotten over you."

She felt herself blushing, as though she were that young and callow again. As though she were as uncertain about how she was supposed to navigate in the world. She managed to say, "Laurie told me. I didn't know. I hadn't heard a word from him in years."

"So maybe this is his way of getting what he wanted all along. Maybe this is his way of compensating for what he's lost that he can't even understand he's lost."

"I'm emblematic," she said.

"Yes . . . of everything he's lost."

"And if he sees me . . ."

"He might see his way back."

᷍᷍ᴗ

A shadow fell across Clare's face, and she opened her eyes to Captain Barnicle's silhouette standing over her. "You can see it now," he said, nodding off over the bow of the ferry.

She rose and stood with him along the railing. The island was still a blue rise on the horizon, a ridge that seemed embossed from the sea itself. From this distance, it was as mysterious as the moon, as untouchable as one of the planets circling in the solar system. But Ledgemere was a place she could touch, a place she had known.

The first time, Riley had taken her in his father's boat. As they approached, he named all the rocks, all the spits of sand. He had told her how the birds came through in their migrations and that year-round islanders used them as calendars in the springtime and the fall. Once, the birds had been the only life to flicker through the forests. There were no chipmunks, no squirrels, no deer or fox. But, two generations back, one of the island boys had married a mainlander, and she had pined for the woodland creatures. As a gift to her, her husband had set about capturing first one animal and then another, and then brought them out by boat, setting them free to range over Ledgemere. "Now the deer eat everyone's gardens," Riley said, "and rightly bear out what the old-timers believe."

"Which is?" she asked.

"That no good can come of importing anything or anybody from the continent." By which he meant Sky Hill and Maine itself and the whole of America.

"Like me," she said.

"Exactly like you," he said. "Here I am, just hauling in trouble."

Whether she was trouble or not, she had loved the island with its red-and-white lighthouse and its magnificent stands of trees and its ragged seashore, which was always being pelted by the sea. Even the sea itself seemed bolder out here. "What do you expect?" Riley had asked. "It's got a clear run all the way from Spain."

Clare had stood on Ledgemere's cliffs in awe of the vertical reach of the Atlantic. It seemed to climb the granite walls, hurl itself as if determined to reach the top, go over it. It cast itself on the rocks, tore itself to shreds, beat itself to foam, and then retreated to give another shove.

In contrast to the relentlessly ravening ocean, the village on the sheltered cove had at once seemed like the very paradigm of coziness. The houses looked as though they had long ago put down roots through the crevices in the mostly stone island. The narrow streets and shingled cottages and weathered fish houses, none of them seemed in the least sturdy, but together they looked as though they could withstand anything—any wind, any rainstorm,

any ice, all time—and still have the petunias spilling out of the
window boxes, still have the yellow lights burning in the windows
at dusk, still have the smoke rising from every chimney.

"It's been a long time," Clare said to the captain. She thought
about how she had dreamed about Ledgemere ever since. It was
one of her dreamscapes, the kind she revisited often in her sleep.
It was always a place of solace.

The captain smiled. "Some people come back every summer.
Feel like they couldn't make it if they didn't come out. Others, I
won't see for years, and then they'll say, 'I needed it this year. I
saved it for when I'd need it.' "

"I can understand that," Clare said. She had wanted to bring
Michael here, to take him by the hand and walk the soft paths
under the fir trees in Worship Forest, where children built fairy
houses out of twigs and moss, where grown-ups left bright copper
pennies at each twig house as an offering for the hardworking
little fairies. She had wanted to lean against him as they sat on
the Gull Wing rocks, high above the surf. She had wanted to. But
never had. Never could. She had never wanted to lay down new
memories over the old. It seemed a desecration. She told the captain: "I always thought I'd come back someday. But I never
wanted to see how it had changed. I wanted it to stay the same."

"It has," he said. "In most ways."

"Good," she said. "Not much does."

"He'll be waiting for you," the captain said.

It startled her that he would get personal, surprised her that he
was thinking of her as anything other than a familiar face who
had turned up on his television set. But he was talking to her, to
the Clare McClendon who had been seventeen and in love with
his friend Billy Brackett's only son, to that girl who had come
back as a woman.

"Riley?" she asked, and when he nodded, she added, "But I
didn't call him."

Captain Barnicle shook his head. "He comes every day. Waits until everyone gets off. Then he asks me, 'Isn't Clare here? Didn't Clare Mac come?'"

"My god," she gasped. "I had no idea. I mean . . . everyone's told me, but I guess I can't really absorb it."

"Who can?" asked the captain. "It's a terrible thing that's happened to Riley Brackett. A terrible thing."

⎯ᏻ᎒⎯

The captain went back to his command, and Clare stood at the railing. She watched as the island rose out of the blue and into its colors: the black-green of its spired firs, the haze of red on the meadow slope where the wild strawberries were ripening in profusion, the russet of the rooftops. Then she watched the colors come into their shapes. There were the gabled summer places high on the land and the clutch of buildings tacked precariously on the narrow streets around the wharf, some of them hanging over the water. There was the inn with its widow's walk and snapping flag. There were the islanders waiting, come down to the ferry for the event of the day: the *Nora B.*'s arrival. There were arms raised in greeting, scissoring back and forth over heads, and finally voices lifting across the water and above the noise of the engine. There was the red of his hair.

Clare hung back. Her sudden and choking impulse was to lurk in the interior of the ferry until it was time for it to turn around and go back to the mainland. She would turn around and go with it. She had been rash to come. She had been bullied by an old lady in a lavender sweater, by a tight-lipped young woman's scorn. But Michael was right. There were some things for which she could offer no remedy. There were some things of which it was better she stay clear. Clearly, this was one of them.

What could she do for Riley? This past year, it had been amply proven to her how vulnerable she herself was. She should not go stumbling into Riley's vulnerabilities. Not even his doctor could say whether it would help or not. In fact, Clare got the impression he was going along with it more for Laurie Brackett's sake than her husband's, and Laurie was going along with it at Mrs. Prentiss's behest, and now Clare was another link in an altogether weak chain of people who didn't know what else to do. The doctor hadn't disguised the fact that he himself thought maybe Riley was in collusion with his injuries.

From inside the *Nora B.,* hanging back in the shade of the concession stand, Clare could see Riley standing in the sunshine and searching the face of each passenger descending the gangway. His concentration was intense. His jaw was set on his hope, firmly. She would have recognized him anywhere. He had not changed, except to be more surely himself. There was more bulk to him. His body had hardened around his long bones, and his face was cast more solidly in its own mold. The devil's thumbprint in his chin was maybe deeper. His hair still swept up from the cowlick on his forehead and hung in ringlets behind his ears. He was burnished with freckles. It looked like a tan from this distance, always had. But she knew that up close, you could see how the freckles overlapped one another—years in the sun, years on the reflective water. More years, since she had touched that skin. More years. Seventeen of them.

The thought snagged her, drew her back to it. She had touched that skin. She had touched him. She had known the taste of his kiss, had ached for his fingertips on her neck and then shuddered when they stroked her, deeply pleased. She had found her own skin with Riley Brackett, found it through his, and finding it had changed her, hadn't it? She had gone on from it, true. She had gone forward. But he had been her first love, the one she had been led to by her flesh and her blood and her nerves, the one who informed her heart and shaped how she would love everyone who came after. He had been first in her heart. And, surfacing from great depth, rising through her consciousness was clear pure memory: of his power over her, the lure of his body for hers, the magnetism of his love.

She should not be here.

Captain Barnicle came for her, reached for her bag. "No," she said. "I can't."

"You can," he said and headed for the door. "You have to."

She could see others still standing, watching the ferry, waiting around the café at the end of the dock. Their eyes were on the boat, even though the ferry passengers had by now trudged past them, up the hill toward the big inn or the boardinghouse or the housekeeping cottages, toward the ocean-view houses rented by the week or the month. The old doorless trucks had already growled up the incline, bearing the luggage that was too heavy to carry and also the supplies ordered by the general store: the boxes of peas and fresh lettuce, the cases of Coca-Cola and Nantucket Nectar, the lemons and oranges. Those old trucks were so far gone that they had already arrived where they were going. Still, everyone watched.

And Clare knew, in a hot flood on her skin, that they were watching for her. She had wandered back into Sky Hill as she would have wandered into it in one of her own dreams. It was happening solely for her. It was her husband who had a sick mother and more on his shoulders than he could bear without bending into it. It was she who had scars under her cotton clothing. It was she who needed to disappear back into a simpler time, to remember how it had been that summer, when she had expected to learn all the worst—separation, death, loss—and instead had learned to live. Two nights ago, sitting there in the Biscuit with her steamed artichoke and scallop chowder, she had thought—no, she had believed—that she could slip back into the skin she had worn that summer and walk, soothed, through the streets of Sky Hill and the trails of Ledgemere Island.

But she was not alone. Riley Brackett was waiting for her, holding his breath for her, and so were the villagers who cared about him and who cared about his wife and his two little barefoot girls. This was not about Clare McClendon.

The captain understood something of what was happening, was at least conscious of the curious spectators. Through the window, she saw him touch Riley on the shoulder, say a few words, and motion with a nod of his head. Riley's eyes flashed to the ferry, and before Captain Barnicle was finished speaking to him, Riley had brushed past him and up the gangway. He came into the sudden shade of the boat, and it was as though he had hit a brick wall. He paused, waiting for his eyes to catch up with his eagerness. And then he saw her.

"Clare," he said. The word had hardly escaped him before he had her in his arms, had crushed her to his chest, had rubbed his face against the close crop of her hair.

She trembled. She began to cry. She wanted so much to be away from him, never to have come.

"You are okay," he said, as if reassuring himself with his own words. "They wouldn't tell me. I thought I'd killed you."

He held her away from him, held her tight on each shoulder so he could look at her. "Your hair," he said. "Did they have to cut it? Oh, Clare Mac, I'm sorry. I'm sorry. Don't cry."

She brought her eyes up to his. There were tears in his too. He was a very familiar stranger. Beautifully familiar. But a stranger. There was so much she had forgotten. More still she had never known about him. Could not have known. They had led separate lives. His touch was almost painful to her.

"Are you okay?" he asked again. "Clare?"

She nodded. It was an effort.

"Let's get outta here," he said, taking her by the hand. She pulled it away. She said, "Riley."

Hurt crossed his eyes. But she could not bear to see herself traipsing up that hill, holding hands with another woman's husband as everyone in the island village watched. What did they expect of her? She could have used a cue from somebody. She wasn't getting one from her heart. All she knew was that she had to protect herself—and him. She had to keep him at a distance. She could not let him get close.

"C'mon," he said.

She wiped her face, composed it into solid lines, and followed him out into the sunlight. He took her bag from the captain's hand and slung it over his own shoulder, and as the two of them headed up the dirt road, he said to the villagers they passed. "Look, it's Clare Mac, good as new." People nodded in acknowledgment, smiled at him, but after his beaming glance had moved away from each one, they swiveled glances at each other, pressed their lips together, or murmured some observation. They were ashamed for him. He was an object of pity.

The way they looked at Clare was level. They did not try to be discreet but clearly meant to measure for themselves whether she would do any good. A crude curiosity glinted in their gazes, though, and she did not miss it. This was clearly the best soap opera to play on Ledgemere Island in years, maybe ever. Tragedy or no, it was something to talk about as they made the twentieth batch of blueberry muffins that month or carried the sheets to the line or scrubbed out the clawfoot tub in a guest's bathroom.

When Riley and Clare reached the first curve in the road, a young woman came down the steps of her porch. The house was a bit off kilter on its foundation, and its cedar shingles were turned a dull gray. Paint peeled on the window trim and on the loose shutters. But her yard was a riot of flowers: snapdragons and foxglove and poppies the color of raspberries. She watched them expectantly.

Riley passed her by, as he had everyone else.

She called after him, "Riley."

He turned. Clare pulled herself up short, looked over her shoulder.

The woman said, "Aren't you going to introduce me?"

Clare saw a grimace twitch at the corners of his mouth. But his voice was kind when he spoke. "She knows who you are," he said, even as Clare tried to recall if she did. Maybe she had years ago, but time had padded itself onto the woman, had blurred the hard lines of her youth. Clare couldn't name her, couldn't even know for sure whether she had ever been able to.

"Do you?" the woman asked.

Clare laughed and said, "I'm sorry, I don't. It's been a while."

"Of course it has, and even then, I don't know that I ever saw you but a time or two. I cleaned rooms then, up at the hotel."

"Oh," Clare said, wishing she had never come, wishing she were back on the ferry, headed to Sky Hill and utter anonymity. "Of course."

"I stayed on the island, married one of the Mapes boys." The woman came closer, extended her hand to Clare. "I'm Kim," she said. "I'm Laurie's sister."

"She doesn't know Laurie," Riley said. He bristled.

"Yes, she does," Kim said. "Don't you?"

Clare nodded. "We've met."

"I'm keeping an eye on Riley here," the woman said. "I make sure he gets enough to eat and all."

"That's nice." What was Clare supposed to say? *Yeah, I get the message. You'll be watching.*

"We've gotta get Clare settled in," Riley said, turning to go. Clare followed his lead.

Kim called after them. "Have a good stay, Clare. I'll be right here if you need anything."

"Thanks so much," Clare called back to her.

"Thanks for nothing," Riley muttered under his breath. His

brow was lowered darkly over his eyes, and not just because of the bright sun.

"I've got a room at the Inn," she told him, when they seemed to have passed through the last of the gauntlet of eyes.

"Same one?" he asked, brightening. "Better be."

"I don't know," she said, remembering suddenly how her room at the Inn had looked down on the carriage house behind his grandmother's cottage, the carriage house that had belonged to Riley from the time he was old enough to claim it. "Mine," he had said. "Mine, mine, mine." His family had still been laughing about his squatter's rights when he was seventeen. But he loved his little house. He slept in a small peaked room upstairs, and downstairs there was a daybed, a table painted the same teal as his lobster markers, and a kitchenette with strawberries stenciled on the cabinets. Out the back door was the shed where he kept the paint for his lobster buoys, and also the extra buoys. They hung under the eaves like Christmas ornaments.

That long ago summer she had spent here, Clare could look down from her room at the Inn to see his bedroom, his window a square of light from the kerosene lamp. The curtains would breathe in and fill with light and then exhale out into the night, glow. He would sit in the window and play his guitar and sing. And she would know it was for her. Probably everybody had known it was for her. The way they loved each other had been no secret even then. Maggie, who ran the Inn and could get away with anything with anybody just because she was practically as old as the island, had once said to Clare, "You wear it like a bridal gown." And when Clare had asked, "What?" Maggie had said, "Your feelings for that damnable Riley."

How could Clare have forgotten how big it had been to him? To her? How could she have taken coming back so blithely? How could she have ignored how much they had once loved each other?

"Didn't you ask?" Riley stopped in the road and looked at her for the answer. He was teasing her, as though they hadn't been apart. Wooling her, as he called it. "Didn't you ask for that room?"

"I forgot," she said. It had been years, she wanted to say. She had forgotten. Not to mention that she was married to someone else who played music for her and that she hadn't thought of their old arrangement in years and this was madness.

He exhaled. "I'll take care of it. Maggie'll do anything for me." He cast a grin back over his shoulder at her as he started up the hill. She wondered if his gait had remained this youthful and eager through the intervening years, or if it was another manifestation of his amnesia. Energy came off him like static electricity.

"You look good to me, Clare Mac," he told her. "Doesn't she look good?" he asked the old man in the red cap who always seemed to be pickaxing some rock in his front yard and was doing it even as they passed.

The old man whistled through his teeth, noncommital. Which was what he would have done seventeen years ago, and Clare realized that only on Ledgemere Island could everything and everyone conspire to make an amnesiac feel at home with the recent years of his memory blown away. Summers came and went and came again, bringing with them the same people engaged in one conspiracy: never to let it change, always to have Ledgemere the way it was.

Nothing had changed. Nothing but Clare herself. And she was beginning to fear that she hadn't changed enough, not enough to make this come out right.

The only place to be alone on Ledgemere was the forest or the cliffs on the far side of the island. And as nervous as Clare was to have to confront Riley one-on-one, she was more undone by the thought of having to confront him with an audience. And in the village, there was an audience. After she had put her bag away in "the" room he had wangled for her, she had gone to a rocker on the front porch to gather her wits and wait for him. Sitting there, she heard one of the coeds who worked at the Inn whisper to another, "That's the one."

Clare smirked to herself. It wasn't lost on her that once she and Riley had come here to have some time to themselves, some time to explore what it was they meant to each other. Now everyone else was exploring it.

She saw him coming across the lawn, wearing a backpack. He was whistling. "Ready?" he asked when he saw her.

"Ready," she said, as much to prompt herself to readiness as anything.

"Trees or waves?"

"Trees, then waves," she answered.

"How did I know you were going to say that?" he asked.

She smiled and fell in next to him as they set off up the hill, where eventually the road would give out and the trail through the forest would begin.

"Thank you," he said.

"For what?"

"I didn't think you'd ever smile at me again. I thought you probably hated me."

"Not me," she said, unsettled by his earnestness. This Riley was a thirty-four-year-old man. He had crinkles at the corners of his eyes and threads of gray twining around the red in his curls, just at his temples. He had arms the size of Michael's thighs. But he also had that power of seriousness, of sincerity that somehow never survived into adulthood. Irony became a necessity then. The young had a gravity that she had forgotten, until she saw it now in him— in relief against what time had done to his body.

"I lost my head," he said. "I knew better." It took her a minute to realize that he was talking about the night of the accident, that night seventeen years ago that had ripped them apart, thrown them out of one another's lives. Almost from the time it had happened, she hadn't let herself think about that night. She wasn't willing to start now. It had been recklessness, hers as much as his.

"I never held it against you," she told him. "I was the one who wanted to see the eclipse."

"Only because I wooled you about going out in the boat," he

said. "About . . ." The skin between his freckles grew red. He was a grown man, blushing like a boy. And she felt herself spark off his embarrassment, off the memory. She felt her skin answer his.

That was the thing about her summer with Riley. He had provoked her with possibilities that she had never even considered before. He had made life seem so much bigger. She had ached to overcome herself, ached to clamber over her own caution and into the fury of being. She had wanted to go where she had never gone before, where she could never go alone, where she could only go with him. That had been the truth of it, no matter what her aunt and uncle thought, or her parents. She hadn't been acting out, as the psychologists would say now. She had been living. For the first time. Maybe too for the last.

"Hurry," he said now, urging her up the road. The open shadow of the woods loomed before them.

"Why?" she asked. She loved this walk and loved to linger over it, always had. How could he have forgotten? If she could remember, surely he could. It amused her, thinking that.

"Hurry," he said again and broke into a run for the next quarter-mile or so. She surprised herself by running after him. But it felt good. She couldn't remember the last time she had actually turned her legs loose and let herself go. Sometimes, staying in the hotel in L.A., for instance, she would run on the treadmill. But that was exercise. That was for her heart and so she wouldn't age too quickly and so she would feel less guilty when she took a bag of potato chips up to her room to eat while watching a late-night *Seinfeld* rerun. It wasn't running. Running was what you did when you were young and couldn't wait to get where you were going.

Riley moved with a long stride up the path and then spurred off onto a deer trail, an obscure course unless you knew it was there, had used it since you were a child. It climbed a rocky hill and came out among the trunks of some of the oldest spruce and fir trees. These trees had never been logged by the early settlers because they were so inaccessible, so high. They seemed primeval.

Clare climbed up after him. "What's the hurry?" she asked, bending over and propping herself up against her knees, pulling in long breaths. She felt good though, felt as if all the tight bonds of anxiety that had been wound up with seeing Riley had come undone and released her back to herself. "What's . . . the . . . big . . . fat . . . hurry?" she teased, mocking her own breathlessness.

"This," he said. He reeled her in to him. He held her close by the waist, and one of his arms ran up her back. With one hand, he held the back of her neck, cradled her like an infant, and looked down into her face. "I was afraid I'd never see you again," he said. "Do you know how afraid I was? It was worse than losing the boat, worse than getting banged around so badly. I thought I had lost you."

"Riley?" she said. It had been years since any man but Michael had held her. The difference ran through her like shivers. She could smell the spice of Riley's skin. She could see how his lips gleamed, could see through the hollow strands of his eyelashes.

He bent to kiss her. "Clare," he said.

She caught herself, freed herself from the moment. Did it belong to now or then? She turned her face away. "Don't," she said.

"Clare Mac," he said.

"You have to listen to me," she began. "I'm not who you think I am."

He laughed with bravado, but fear flared up in his eyes. He had been through this before in the months since his head trauma. Somebody was always saying something that didn't make sense to him. Somebody was always trying to prove him wrong. And he wasn't having any part of it. Not from her. Not now. "Is your name Clare Mac?" he asked with a burr of defiance in his voice.

She hesitated, then nodded.

"Did I push you off the bridge into the inlet, and that's how we met?"

She nodded.

"Did I kiss you in the bathroom at the Biscuit because you finally agreed to go out with me, and then I couldn't stand it because I wanted a taste of you, and I followed you, and you got flustered at first, but then you let me in there with you and you let me kiss you right there with the toilet still running and then you didn't want me to stop?"

This time she laughed, couldn't check herself.

"Are you the Clare Mac who can't stand to be kissed there . . ."—he touched the hollow of her breastbone, and she began to turn away from his fingertips—". . . because you're ticklish?"

She circled away from him, walked a few steps deeper into the trees.

His voice was hushed now, and insistent. It pressed against her as his flesh had only minutes earlier. "Are you the girl who walked across the grass at the Inn in the middle of the night and threw a piece of shell through my open window, which thunked me between the eyes? And then when I hung out the window to see what was going on, aren't you the one who said, 'I love you?' Aren't you that Clare Mac?"

She closed her eyes but felt his on her like the lights of the television camera. They demanded something of her, demanded that she rise to them.

"Clare Mac?" he pressed. "Aren't you?"

"Race you to the lagoon," she said and sprinted off into the trees, following her memory and his old lead, running away, too, from her memory and from him.

He had known the way through this forest and had shown her its secrets. The summer people tended to stay on the numbered hiking trails. In fact, the trail maps warned hikers off the "deer trails." Riley had told her before, with a wry smirk, "We've got to keep something for ourselves."

One of the things the islanders had kept for themselves was the high lagoon, a pool of fresh water hemmed by trees and cliffs on one side and by the cliffs and the ocean on the other. It was green from its great depth, and someone long ago, probably the wife of some captain who had been in the China trade on one of the great old schooners, had named the place Jade. Clare dreamed she was swimming in it sometimes, that she saw her body yellow in the green water, suspended and serene and safe. She ran toward it now.

"Wrong way," Riley yelled from behind her, and when she turned, he had already branched off onto the true trail, and by the time she reversed herself, she was falling farther and farther behind him. He had strength in his legs, and he far outpaced her. At times, she could hear him better than she could see him.

The air in the forest was sweet with balsam. Invisible birds chittered in the high fronds, and always on this side of the island was the stirring surge of the surf. It roared on rougher days than this, but even now it was something alive around them, a witnessing presence. Like what she believed God might be.

Looking down at the path, she bore herself up. Her feet found their grounding between the round stones, on the gnarled roots of trees that lent themselves as staircases. The muscles in her legs stretched and held, stretched and held. She grew hot with the work and was silent except for her breath, and it came in and out of her like the rush of the water. Blood too murmured in her ears. She smelled her skin as it grew moist. She climbed. Feeling strong, she climbed.

She glanced ahead to judge where she was, and she saw him, limned in sunlight, broken out at last onto the precipitous edge of

Jade. He held out his hand to her as she stepped into the sunlight, onto the jutting rock. The ocean was a clamor of blue beyond the green lagoon. It crashed below them, throwing itself up the side of the cliffs, hissing white, retreating for another surge. In contrast, Jade lay still, a pool of water suspended between their height and the ocean farther down, a mirror of the sky and the circling birds and two small figures: his and hers.

He beckoned with his fingers. "Come on," he said impatiently. His hand waited, outstretched.

Sloughing her bag off her shoulder and casting it down on the rock next to his backpack, she closed the gap between them. She was breathing deeply, flushed with the climb. Still, she did not reach for him.

"You've gotta jump while you're still climbing," he urged her.

She took his hand. And he led her over the edge. Still dizzy with climbing fast, they leapt, then fell. Color streaked around them, liquid. All sound became wind. It happened forever—his fingers around hers, squeezing; the glance of her eyes off his; the last long-drawn breath; reaching for her nose. Then the weight of him pulled them apart finally. She shut her eyes, heard the water close around him. And then it took her.

She felt the cold as heat at first, a scorch of motion. The fear rose up in her throat, and she kept her eyes closed on it and held her breath to spite it, and she kept sinking sinking sinking until her body hung suspended in a depth she couldn't let herself acknowledge. It hung as if caught there, and then it began to rise. She opened her eyes and saw the light above her, saw it through the shadows, the green distortion of light. She broke through it finally, shattered through—it seemed nothing but a surface. But she rose into it. Light surrounded her as the water had. She reached for her first breath, swallowed it.

Riley kissed her then, when the air was still new in her lungs, burning. He closed his warm mouth around hers. She tasted him, felt the rough pleasure of his tongue, the solidity of his arms around her. She felt the rush of him in her blood, felt her skin slipping along the length of him, her legs caught up in his. They went under, breathing the kiss, taking in each other and water and air. He held onto her as though onto life, and she clung to him.

And when they surfaced, time righted itself, and she knew who she was and where. And when.

"Please," she said, pulling away. "Oh God, Riley, please. I can't."

She stroked for the rocks that piled up out of the water, a natural ladder leading up to the warm shelf where the sun fell hard and steadily. She clambered up to it.

"I don't understand," he said, following her.

She emptied the water out of her shoes, furious at herself for, among other things, not kicking them off. If she had to go in for the same risky leaps as she had gone in for as a kid, at least she could have used her adult common sense.

"I don't understand."

Wringing the water from the leg of her shorts, she said, "I know you don't."

He sat down next to her, dropped himself really. She thought it must have hurt to land that hard. But he seemed beyond knowing what his body felt. He was all up in his eyes. He was confusion.

"I shouldn't have come back," she said. "I'm not going to do you any good."

"Don't talk like that," he said. "Of course you had to come back. I love you. We love each other. It was just an accident. We can go on from here. Everything..."

"Riley," she said, disbelieving the situation, though she didn't disbelieve him. She didn't. No one would be so brash. No one who was as good as Riley at heart.

"I love you," he said.

She sighed. "I know you think you do," she said. "But I'm not the same person. You're not the same person." She looked him in the eye, reached for his hand to hold onto him while she said what she had to say. "Riley, that was seventeen years ago."

He leaned back his head and laughed, which was not at all what she had expected.

"Not for me," he said. "I don't care what everyone keeps saying. Not for me. I can't."

"Riley, you have to look at the facts."

"I can't," he said.

"You have to. It's the way the world works."

"Not mine," he told her, as he snapped to his feet in what seemed one motion. "It's not the way my world works, Clare Mac. My world is here." He grabbed his head in his hands, held them there, grew still. "In here."

And then, he dropped his arms, as if losing his grip on his own spirit. He turned away from her, toward the forest and the trail-head. His skin was still glistening with the water from the lagoon. "Don't you love me?" he asked. He waited for her to answer.

"No," she said. "I don't."

The muscles of his face collapsed as though she had struck the feeling from them. "You're lying," he said.

She felt terrible, tried to ease him: "It's not a question of love, Riley. It doesn't matter who feels what. It's a question of what's real and what's not. What can *still* be real and what cannot." She waited for his response; none came. With tenderness, she said, "I have a life I have to go back to and so do you. That's real."

"You wanna know what's real, Clare?" he asked. "What's real is that I love you. That's the only real thing. That's the only thing I know right now. The only thing." He disappeared into the shade.

For a minute or two, she heard his feet, squeaky in their wet shoes, and then there was only the sound of the ocean tormenting itself on the rocks and the racket of the gulls crying foul in the sky, and there was only Clare herself on a shelf of rock looming over a pool of green water, so still now in the sun. Too still. Too far out of the currents of time.

Part Two

When Clare stopped talking, JoJo was feeding a pigeon that was two steps below them on the cascade of stairs outside the Metropolitan Museum of Art. She paused, with a pinch of pretzel poised, and looked over at Clare, who was staring at the bird. City gulls, Clare was thinking.

"He just kissed you?" JoJo asked. "*Kissed* you, kissed you?"

Clare nodded.

"Oh my god, Clare, what did you do then?"

Clare shrugged. "I ate a lobster roll," she said.

"I mean about Riley."

"I know what you mean. But it was just overload, you know. All I could do was walk back to the Inn and sit at a table in the dining room and stare out the window. I just wanted to be empty. I just wanted to be nothing more than what I could see."

Clare looked over at JoJo to see if her friend understood, but all she could see was herself reflected starkly in the dark lenses of Jo's sunglasses. She looked big-eyed, naive, not equal to telling her own story. She sighed and said, "I was just worn out already."

She told JoJo how she had looked up that evening to see the innkeeper coming toward her. Maggie had a bowl in her hands: her specialty, dessert. "Thought you looked like a girl who could use a sweet," Maggie said, sitting down in the chair across from Clare—crashing down into it, really.

Clare smiled in greeting and said, "Sure."

Maggie hadn't changed much. She was older, of course, but wore ninety years much as she had worn seventy-three. Her thin feet were loose in purple rubber clogs, and her white hair was sticking out in wild, if wispier, curls from beneath a weathered captain's hat that had a sweat stain at the band. Maggie still worked, the dining-room hostess had told Clare earlier when they were chatting over the menu. In fact, Maggie still worked hard. She set out a dozen lobster traps most days and grew vegetables for the dining room, coaxed tomatoes and peppers and cucumbers up out of "this old rock," as she called Ledgemere Island. Clare noticed now that her hands were still strong, though the skin was worn see-through and rubbed brown in spots.

"It's a shame about Riley getting hit between the face and eyes," Maggie had said without preliminary niceties. She was chewing on a toothpick. "You'll straighten him out, though. If anybody can. Eat some more of this shortcake. You won't get strawberries like that in New York. Sour soil down there. Not enough ocean salt."

While Clare ate double helpings, each with a scoop of vanilla bean ice cream, Maggie told her some more things she hadn't known about Riley and almost wished she didn't ever have to know. What was the old lobsterwoman's motive in telling her? Or was it just island talk? Was it just the old rainy-day fallback of storytelling?

Maggie had always kept a notebook by the fireplace in the hotel's gathering room. It was called the Ledgemere Novel, and any guest who wanted to could add his or her own chapter. As far as Clare knew, no islander, not even Maggie herself, ever picked up that notebook. It was merely an inclement-weather amusement for the paying guests: a calculated condescension. Let them think someone cared what had happened to them on Ledgemere. Really, the islanders themselves had always preferred the stories that belonged only to them. They seemed never to tire of telling each other what they already knew. Recycling, Clare thought. Island people were thrifty by nature.

After supper, Clare felt mired in what Maggie had revealed. Restless, she left the inn and walked through the village and out onto the eastern edge of the island. She had always been nervous coming to this rough strand. In the last century, two children, a brother and sister, had been swept away while playing here. The surf was unpredictable, lapping away at the outer rocks, then suddenly licking high, reaching far, swallowing. Even now, all these years later, Clare stayed high on the shore, hugging the tree line.

A merchant ship had been wrecked here after the Second World War, and its rusted hull lay in pieces on the rocks, scattered like a child's broken toys. Tonight there were children climbing on it, chattering like seabirds. But as the sun sank behind the island and the sky grew red as embers and then purple, the children disappeared into the paths among the tall grasses. They went back to the beach houses where the windows were warm with kerosene light and where their parents sat like silhouettes at the screened porch windows, watching the night come on. After they were gone, Clare was alone.

She didn't know where Riley was. Maggie hadn't mentioned his absence, nor had anyone else, and Clare hadn't dared to ask. She was glad of his disappearance, really, relieved. After what had happened, she felt almost dizzy. Time seemed to have become liquid around her at Jade; it seemed to have run upstream. Seeing her hadn't brought Riley back to the present. If anything, their afternoon together had swept her back to the past, back to him.

Clare kept seeing the look on Riley's face when she had tried this afternoon to talk about the recent past, about the years that were denied him. What had that look been in his eyes?

Not anger purely, nor simply denial. Betrayal was closest, she thought. She had betrayed him. After all, he still felt about her as she had felt about him that summer seventeen years ago. He still felt love as something that woke him in the night, something that sang in his blood. He loved her with his whole body, she was sure of it. Today she had remembered what that had been. She had remembered what it was to love him that way, to sense him through the soles of her feet and at the roots of her hair and all down her spine. To want him. To need him.

That was the thing about their love. It had been first. They found each other at a time when they were ripe to discover themselves. Wasn't that what so much of it was? Looking back, she thought that she hadn't been herself really until she had been with Riley. He had shown her corners of herself she hadn't even suspected of existing. He had given her, in so many ways, the gift of herself. Before him, she had never known what her body could feel. So naturally, when Riley touched her and she felt something like lightning jar through every nerve, she had ascribed its energy to him. She had thought he was the source of the power, that he was the only one who could make her float above herself and go deep inside her own body and farther beyond it than she had ever gone.

She had plummeted through sheer island air with him, free.
She had gone far out to sea. She had absorbed sunlight as never
before, had felt the weight of water cupped in her palms. She had
heard gulls and high wind through fir trees, had heard them so
intensely that it felt as if she were being brushed by the sounds
themselves, as if they had a texture she could discern with her
fingertips. Back then, she had noticed poppies growing along the
road, had seen them fired with a vibrance that she was sure had
never been there before. Love had changed the way she lived in
the world. Riley had.

But that power had been coming from herself, hadn't it? She
had left the island and Maine that summer, and the power had
gone with her, that ability to come alive at someone's touch. She
had loved another boy in college, so much that she had thought
she would marry him. Which was when she learned that she loved
her own possibilities more. After that, she had moved to New
York alone and had learned to rely on herself, had savored the
satisfaction of that. As much as she and JoJo had bemoaned their
mostly paltry romances, she had often thought, *I know how to make
myself happy*. And she had. The job had sometimes made her miserable, as had the burden of trying to get by in the city. Still, she
felt whole.

And then she met Michael. It was as if her experience multi-
plied times two. He doubled her, extended her pleasure, her hope-
fulness, but also her vulnerabilities: Anything that hurt him could
hurt her as deeply. She had called it love and believed it to be
love. She had believed it would endure.

If Riley had ever had that, if he had ever been whole in himself,
if he had ever had his joy increased by his wife or by his daughters,
if any of that had ever happend to him, it was lost to him now.
Clare did not know enough about the past two decades to discern
the truth. Somehow, he had bought a fancier lobster boat and

married a girl who had gone to the same high school, and he had fathered two children. Clare had only other people's words that he had never "gotten on." That's how Maggie had put it.

Maggie had told her that once Riley and Laurie had brought their little girls into the inn for a special dinner. It was probably their wedding anniversary, Maggie thought, and as they were eating, Mandy leaned over and whispered to her dad that Clare Mac was sitting across the room. Riley hadn't even been able to swallow what was in his mouth.

It had been a teenage girl who did look uncannily like Clare, Maggie said. Everyone agreed that she was almost a twin. And Riley had stared at her a minute, then gotten up from the table and walked out of the room. He didn't come back in, not even for dessert, which said a lot. "And that was before he got whacked between the face and eyes," Maggie said. "He just never got on. Think about it. How many men do you know whose five-year-old daughter could recognize his first girlfriend? You think about it."

—⌒⌒⌒—

JoJo flung her weight forward, rested on her knees, whistled out a long breath. She said, "I'm sorry, Clare, but don't you think that's creepy?"

"It's unnerving," Clare admitted. "Still, it's sad too, don't you think?"

JoJo nodded. "Of course, I do. But I have to tell you, if it had been me, I would've been out of there. I mean, it's not your problem. You tried, right?"

"That night, I just felt so heavy with it. And I just wanted to get away. I just wanted morning to come so I could load up on that ferry and go back to Sky Hill and race home."

"But...?" JoJo swung a penetrating look over at Clare, interrogated her.

Clare paused, tried to find an equation of words that would make JoJo feel what she had gone through. "But it started being not just about Riley. It started being about me. And about Michael. And about everything that's happened..."

~❧

After night had closed in around the island and the Milky Way was
strewn across the sky like a flimsy veil, Clare had gone back to
her room. It was early for sleep, but she couldn't concentrate on
reading, and finally she had turned off the light and lain with her
head propped up, watching the lace curtains breathe in and out,
watching the stars beyond.

The heavens were brighter here than anywhere else she had
ever been. It was because of the darkness, how pure it was out
here in the ocean, far from the strung electricity of the mainland,
the trapped orange haze of civilization. She had read that in New
York City you could only see about a dozen stars, and in the
suburbs maybe five hundred. Light pollution, the astronomers

called it. At Kidd Peak outside Tucson, even with their high-power telescopes, they had been forced to give up the search for the farthest galaxies.

It occurred to Clare that humans were learning how to turn night into day, conquering the dark itself instead of their fear of it. But they were blinding themselves to the universe, insulating themselves from the big questions, the potential answers. There were fewer and fewer places left on Earth from which to see the night sky, from which to observe star clusters and pulsars, from which to take comfort in the constancy of the constellations and the other planets in their certain orbits around the shared sun. At least Ledgemere was one of the places where the sky still had its majesty, its mystery: this celestial brightness nothing but a gift of the utterly black sea grasping endlessly at the island's shores, a gift of a black sea lured by the moon's green-gold attraction.

She understood how light depended on darkness now, as she understood that the stars were nothing but cosmic bodies of hot glowing gas, light years away, their sparkle nothing but the escaped energy of nuclear fusion. And far from being randomly cast beauty, they were each assigned their place in the constellations, in the vast universe. They were charted by astronomers for their brightness and their temperature—the red giants and the super giants, the black and white dwarfs. A fairy tale in the sky. Oh, Be a Fine Guy, Kiss Me. That's how she had learned to remember the spectral classifications. O was the hottest, M the coolest. The sun was an M. Now she understood something of the science of the sky.

Last time she had seen the stars from Ledgemere, they were merely the magic of her own emotions, the scattered sparks of her own passion and Riley's. Sometimes the two of them had lain in the grass below this window, on the knoll between his carriage house and her room, and they had watched the sky together. She could remember being on her back in the cool grass and he on his next to her, touching only one another's fingertips. It had been as though she were plugged in to electricity, just by that merest touch. It was as though the two of them made the stars blaze that way.

How could she blame him for loving what they had been to each other? She too loved it. She had simply forgotten it. She had simply lived past it. Gotten on.

From below, she heard the guitar, and the pace of her heart caught on it. The sound of it was familiar still. He was a simple player, had taught himself. But there was a fluidity to his playing that was all his own. Often, he made it up as he went along. She had only found that out because she had once asked him to play something again, something she had loved. "Sorry," he had said sheepishly. "I can't."

"You can't?"

"It only happens to me once. Sorta like waves. You know they keep coming, and technically they're the same water, pulled by the same moon, but they're different every time."

After that, she would ask him to play her some waves, and she guessed that's what he was doing now, all these years later, down in the carriage house behind his grandmother's place. Clare didn't get up from the bed to look, but she knew if she did it would be dark, and his curtains would be caught in the breeze as hers were, and there would be no sign of him except his music: playing waves.

Maybe he was playing for himself. Maybe he was playing for her. Anyway, it was mournful music, unlike anything she had ever heard him play before. Listening to it, she understood that Riley was full of a melancholy that no seventeen-year-old could know, certainly not the buoyant seventeen-year-old he had been. He may have lost his consciousness of his past. But he had not lost his past. It was there in him, keening out in his music, telling him stories he might not understand, telling her.

It had been Riley, all those years ago, who had opened her to music, to what was unspoken but eloquent. Growing up, she had mostly heard music with words: hymns at church, her mother's beloved show tunes on the hi-fi, her father's folk songs. She had always thought the words were what was important, not the music. Not the meaning of the music itself. Until Riley. It was Riley who taught her to understand that more could be passed between two people without words. It must have been Riley too who prepared her for Michael, though she had never realized it. Not until now.

Michael had played for her often, early in their relationship. The first time, he had taken her to Juilliard, where he had spent years as a student. The two of them could have gone to the music shop on Fifty-seventh Street, where he had a job playing the Steinways and selling them on commission. He could have taken her to the hotel where he played most teatimes and evenings. But he had wanted what neither of those options afforded: intimacy. Time out of time.

At Juilliard, there were soundproof practice rooms. Michael took her into one and closed the rest of the world out. He had her stand with her hands on the piano. "Close your eyes," he had said. "Close your eyes, Clare." And she had.

He played pianissimo at first, so very softly. It was just a vibration, she remembered, almost nothing but a shadow of music. It entered her, slipped in. And then it began to rise out of her, beyond her, and it became the space in which they existed. They were no longer inside the white institutional space with padded walls where other students had played other songs. They were in a place of his conjuring, a place made of shifting light, of green and purple and yellow, a place where every color had its voice and its texture, even its taste. It was a place of distant reaches, yet intimacy. It was hers, made for her.

"Could you smell it?" he asked when he had finished playing and had come to stand with his hands over hers.

Without opening her eyes, she had leaned into him and kissed him and known that they would be together. She had known that she needed to be with Michael because he could take her outside herself and also into him with nothing more tangible than vibration quivering in wires. He could build safe places, enduring places, with nothing but evaporating sound.

Even working two jobs, he had never been able to buy the only kind of piano he had ever wanted. So it had been her wedding gift to him. She had asked one of the researchers at the network to call Michael at the shop and masquerade as a wealthy woman special-ordering a piano, someone who didn't know anything about music except that the man she loved could play beautifully. "Tell him you want the one he would buy for himself if he could. The best. Money is no object," Clare told the researcher.

Michael had done as instructed, and it had incurred for Clare a rather sizable debt, as well as wiping out her savings. But nothing could have given her more pleasure than to spend on Michael the money that she had made "getting paid for daylight." That's what she and JoJo had called working overtime. The network had paid them well to work fourteen to sixteen hours a day, to give up weekends if necessary. One summer, she figured the network paid her for every single hour of daylight. She never saw the city in the sunshine except walking to the subway from her apartment and from the subway to the office for about ten minutes each morning. "No danger of melanoma this year," she had told JoJo one midnight when they came down the twenty-seven floors in the elevator together.

It was worth it to her, spending all that money. It was worth it just for that moment on the Saturday before their wedding when Michael's hauling buddies from the shop on Fifty-seventh Street delivered the beautiful piano. He had stood speechless in the apartment, wearing only khaki shorts and green high-top tennis shoes. "You should not have done it," Michael insisted after the guys had toasted him with the champagne their boss had sent along. He waited for the guys to leave, and then he said it had to go back, adding with a smile, "even though it will mean giving back the commission on it," which, much to her secret delight, he had been crowing about for two weeks. "We're sending it back. I'm sure we can arrange it."

"No way," she had told him. "I spent a lot of daylight earning that piano. And now when I need sunshine, you'll play it for me."

And he had. The piano had loomed in their Brooklyn apartment, which was the parlor floor of a once-opulent old brownstone. Their bedroom had formerly been the parlor, and the living room had been the music room. The plaster on the ceiling still had lutes and harps in bas-relief, ornate and Victorian, like something out of Edith Wharton. The Steinway fitted perfectly, gleaming in its polished splendor. It seemed they were living in luxury, if you ignored the galley kitchen carved into one end of the room, and the closet-size bathroom with the pipes that screamed.

Many nights, the worst nights, the ones when someone spiked her self-confidence at the office or the subway stalled for two hours under the East River or she dreamed that her mother was alive and she then lost her all over again, on those nights, Michael played sunshine for her. Sometimes he'd get up after midnight and find her sitting in her rocking chair, rocking herself, hugging herself, hurting. Then he would play for her, softly softly softly, music that was surreptitious as the shadows of leaves under an oak tree, and she would believe in daylight despite darkness.

Looking out the window at Ledgemere's stars, Clare realized that Michael had not played for her in a long time. The piano had its own room in the cottage on the Hudson, the baby's room. What could have been the baby's room, but now never would. The piano had filled the space there. But somehow it had not occupied the same place in their lives as it had in the Brooklyn apartment.

It seemed outside their lives. It seemed not to belong, seemed to be usurping what—who—should rightfully have shared their home.

The last time she could remember him playing was the night they had found out about the possibility of her cancer. She had gone for a checkup at his urging, had rushed home from Washington on the shuttle to keep the appointment. She had wanted to do everything right—the vitamins, the folic acid, no wine with dinner while they were trying to conceive. "Okay," she had told him. "I'll make sure everything's in good working order. For you." But it had been as much for her.

She had thought, finally, that they had found a way to make a start even in the midst of an ending, even in the long years of Belle's illness: a baby. Michael had quickened at the thought, had seemed hopeful again for the first time in years. But it had been the beginning of only another ordeal.

A lump. Maybe nothing. She had lain in bed that night, and the lump had grown into its horrifying potential. She had gotten up and gone to the parlor and curled into a corner of the couch because she was shaking and did not want to wake him. As she sat there, drawn up on her dread, she had heard the music. He was playing for her. It started low, hushed, the way she loved it. But it began to swell and then burst in its swelling. It began to crash.

She trembled from it and went on her bare feet to stand in the doorway of the piano room. Even in the moonlight, she could see the tears on his face, the anger. Crossing to him, she laid her hands on his, and the music thudded, clabbered, stopped with an off-key hum that continued for long minutes to vibrate between them, off the walls and ceiling. "Michael," she said.

He turned to her and put his face between her breasts and sobbed. His mouth moved against her flesh in silent anguish. In squelched screams, he said to himself what he could not say to her—not then in his spilling sorrow, not ever.

Since then, he had not touched their piano, not in her presence at least. There was no daylight in darkness in their home on the river. Hadn't been for a long time. Wouldn't be, either, for as far ahead as she could see.

℘

Riley still played below, stroked out sorrow on a battered acoustic guitar. And Clare lay upstairs in the hotel room, curled around her pain. Around hers and around Michael's and around Riley's.

Tomorrow she would go. The midday ferry would come, and she would be on it when it left. She would leave Riley to his limbo. She would go back to her life. To her own limbo. To Michael's.

Morning was incandescent beyond her eyelids. She had to squint into the new day, but the light blazing down from the sun and reflecting off the unbroken reaches of the ocean seemed a force that entered her, a charge. Even while she was still stretching in bed, her plan was to dash down to the landing and buy a cappuccino at the sandwich shop. Fancy coffee seemed to be the island's one concession to contemporary culture, and she was feeling the urge. The jolt of caffeine would match her sudden mood.

Then she would sit on the hotel's front porch and call Michael. Cell phones didn't work out here on the island, she'd found. The only option was the pay phone by the front door, which didn't offer much privacy. In fact, one of her favorite pastimes as a teenager had been eavesdropping on the one-sided dramas of people talking on the phone. It didn't matter what the truth was or wasn't. She filled in the gaps, made the story her own. Instant entertainment.

So she'd give some kid a thrill. Although she wasn't sure how scintillating her conversation with Michael could possibly be. Is your mother's digestion any better? Did you get Del's house on the market? Is the new prescription helping with the agitation? Clare had been avoiding even thinking about it. Maybe, too, she'd been avoiding having to talk to Michael, having to hear the whole of his untouchable pain, hear it echoing in his voice, hear how far he was from her in every way. Had it been two days or three since she had spoken to him?

When she came downstairs into the aroma of bacon and eggs, Riley was walking in the screen door of the front lobby. He had a brown bag balanced on the palm of his hand. "I bet you'd drink a cappuccino," he said.

A fresh start, she thought. Something that had no link to their past. She smiled slowly at him, thanking him wordlessly. "I've been known to," she said, noticing how casual his manner seemed in contrast to the day before. She did her best to follow his lead.

"Good," he said, "because I've brought you a cup and . . ."—a grin spread from one corner of his mouth—". . . Maggie's letting us use the *Lily* . . . if you're up for it."

She considered telling him that she was headed back to Sky Hill today, that she didn't have time to go out on the boat, that she had tried . . . But the words didn't come. And the thought crossed her mind: *Why not stay? what are you rushing away to? to whom?*

This morning the island had caught her up in the nets of its old and simple sorcery: clothes hung out on a line between two windows, the cries of birds over the harbor, the sight of the light-house on the hill cleaved in two by light and shadow. She was not ready to leave. Not yet. Not after all the time away. Why should she hurry away when she was peaceful for once? The sun was shining. The monkshood were blooming blue, and the air smelled of warm balsam needles.

"Decaf or caf?" she asked, playing that her decision hung on the answer.

"Both," he said, and shrugged sheepishly. "I bought one of each and thought I'd drink what you didn't want."

The *Lily* was an old vessel, but Riley referred to it fondly as a hooker: a good, sturdy workboat. Maggie had long ago festooned it with gull feathers and shells strung on fishing line. The seat cushions were covered in faded floral chintz, making the whole affair appear somewhat Laura Ashley. One thing about Maggie, Clare thought as she clambered out of the tender and into the lobster boat, she would work within sight of the men from way before dawn until she had her haul. She would hoist ninety yards of strung traps overboard and spit in the sea between her front teeth and come home reeking of redfish bait. But she would not deny her femininity.

Riley stood inside the pilothouse at the helm, and he turned the boat out into the sun, out into the open ocean. Clare perched herself on the roof, looking out from under the brim of her straw hat, breathing the steam from her cappuccino. For such a cloudless day, the seas were rough, a fact she noticed when they came out of the harbor. It gave her a sense memory that made her shudder, and she was suddenly surprised at herself for agreeing to this at all. Any fear must have been overcome by the old magnetism.

A salt spray sheered over the sides, sparkling. The boat nosed into the waves heavily, rolling sometimes so that Clare had to hold tightly to the edge of the cap. Soon she gave it up entirely and headed back to the stern. On her way past, she grinned at Riley, and he said, "Better stay in here with me. It'll get wet back there."

"I need the sun," she demurred, and she thought she did need it. These past days, the sunlight seemed almost to be reviving something in her. She believed there was no place like Maine for an undiluted quality of light. No place like Ledgemere and its waters. The allure of Los Angeles had been lost on her in the last few months of living there. Every morning, the city woke up swaddled in fog, and the sun, when it finally burned through, was only a high, indeterminate glare. It seemed to be everywhere and yet come from nowhere, blinding. And even the Hudson River valley, which had lured her out of the city with its rugged beauty, even there, the light got diffused through heavy moist air. It was muffled. But on Ledgemere, the light was so pure it seemed to ring.

From the back of the *Lily,* Clare watched Riley. The morning sun falling through the windshield cast his shadow long, so long that she could have reached out and put her hand into it, as into a pool of water. He was dressed in a faded blue polo shirt that had come untucked from the back of his jeans. The long sleeves were pushed up over his elbows, and the hair on his forearms stood out like an aura in the bright sun. The high round-toed rubber boots reached up his calves. She remembered him wearing them when she had known him before. They made him look boyish, always had. Where she had grown up, only little boys had worn rubbers on their way to and from school on torrentially rainy days. So she had been charmed from the first.

At the helm of the *Lily,* Riley had a sure hand. He had skippered his daddy's boat since he could whistle "Yankee Doodle Dandy," a coincidence that had lodged in his mind and that he had repeated to her that first time he took her out in the boat. She had been nervous then—no, she had been *terrified* of the ocean, having been warned of the rogue waves that swept away unsuspecting beachcombers. Aunt Fran had told her a cautionary anecdote the first time Clare had asked whether she was allowed to go with Riley to Ledgemere. "The Atlantic has taken people from high on the rocks out there, swept them clear away. It's capricious," she said, then added, almost surreptitiously, "same as Riley."

That was as much warning as her aunt had ever given her about the ocean or Riley Brackett. Uncle Tig had, characteristically, stayed quiet. Every once in a while, there were little cautionary bells that went off in Clare's own head, set off by her own solid and good sense, but even these began to be part of the cacophony of being with him, the frenzy in her blood. Beneath all that, she had trusted him. She had trusted him because of one moment.

After the night he had pushed her off the bridge and then followed her home, they had flirted with each other violently for several weeks. There had been a one-upmanship, almost a glorying in the other's discomfort. He had come to the library and pretended to read *Great Expectations,* though really he was watching her provocatively over the top of it. She glued pockets into new books and blushed in a hot and red rash that crept up her neck and burned in her ears. In retaliation, when she saw him making a lobster delivery to the Prentisses, she volunteered to take the bouquet up for the dining-room vase. While there, she told Mrs. Prentiss, in Riley's presence, how he was "devouring" the Dickens novel. "Oh," said Mrs. Prentiss in delight as she turned to Riley with great expectations of her own. "Tell me what you think of Pip?" Riley had stammered and burned his singular shade of scarlet.

It might have gone on that way—joust, counterjoust—if Riley had not stalked her to the bridge late on another day. It was gray, melancholy weather. The fog was coming up the harbor like a stealthily advancing army, and she was watching it. After spying her sitting on the railing, Riley had parked his truck at a distance and crept up behind her. He had reached to push her over. As his hand touched the hollow between her shoulders, she turned. There were tears streaming down her face. Scrambling, he tried to undo what he had already begun. He grabbed at her clothes as she began to fall. He strained to hold her. But she fell anyway.

It seemed to her later that he was down the side of the embankment before she surfaced. As she came to her sputtering senses, he was plunging in after her. "Clare," he said, reaching for her. "I didn't know. I didn't know you were upset."

Turning away from him, she charged for the other side, climbing the rocks. He was behind her. "Please," he said.

She swung a leg over the seat of her bicycle, cocked her foot on the pedal, leaned to go. He caught her by the arm.

"What is it?" he said. "What's wrong?"

Shaking her head, as if to shake him off, as well as her own dark thoughts, she put her weight on the pedal, began to roll.

"Who else are you going to tell?" he called after her.

Slowing, she waited for more.

"Clare?"

She turned as he walked up beside her.

"What's wrong?" he asked, laying his hand next to hers on the handlebar.

Clare measured him with her gaze. When she spoke, she felt almost spiteful. She knew her words were a weapon. "My mother," she told him. "She's dying."

It was his reaction that made her heart turn at last toward his, take him in. It was his reaction that made her rebuke herself for having wanted to shame him with her grief. His nostrils flared suddenly, as though her words were a blast of hot air in his face. His eyes began to gleam with tears. He swallowed hard.

"I'm sorry," he said. And he reached to hold her. She let him. It was the first time they had ever touched one another in tenderness. "I'm sorry," he said into her wet hair.

They stood there in silence for some minutes. The fog stole

around them, closed them in together. They might have turned to stone on that road, stunned at their sudden proximity. They might have, if Riley had not shifted his weight and squished in his boots. That had made her laugh.

_G>G_

"Okay," Riley said now, reeling her back in from her reflections. He was still standing in the shade of the pilothouse. She couldn't see his features.

Looking at the sky, she guessed they had been skimming across the water now for maybe an hour. The boat was quieter, she noticed. It was no longer applying itself against the long swells of the ocean. Instead, it bucked back and forth on the rough water, seemingly at each wave's mercy.

"Okay?" she echoed, looking up at him expectantly.

He stepped out into the sunshine. The engine was idling with a steady bubbling sound.

"What are we doing?" she asked. She stood and turned a complete circle, scanned nothing but the line of the horizon. The boat nosed over a swell and fell. She caught herself on the railing. "Should it be this rough on a sunny day?"

"It pays attention to the moon and the stars," he said, coming toward her. "Not the sun. You know that."

She giggled, but a tension was knotting itself up along her spine as he approached. "I learned that the hard way," she said, teasing him.

His mouth twisted into an odd smile, but he seemed nervous and intent on her, so intent he couldn't be distracted by humor. He sought her eyes with his. "Clare," he began, "seeing you sitting back here . . ." He didn't know how to—or wouldn't allow himself—to finish. She saw the knot of his Adam's apple slide down, then up again as he swallowed the rest of his thought.

Why was he doing this? Annoyance spiked in her. He was ruining it. She had finally felt comfortable with him again. She had finally been within range of where he was, within range of where she thought she might be able to help him.

He stood in front of her and looked at her searchingly. "Don't you remember?" he asked.

She squinted up at him.

He looked out over the water.

"What, Riley?"

"It's just that I'm not the only one who's forgotten something. Am I?"

"Don't," she said softly. "Please, Riley, don't."

His hands came toward her, and it seemed to her they came in a slowed form of motion. She flinched inwardly at his touch but managed to keep it from rippling out where he would feel it. Her mind raced around in its dark corners, searching for a way to fend off his tenderness without hurting him. Without hurting him, the thought was loud inside her. Why was he putting her in this position?

It seemed whole minutes passed as his hands touched her elbows and moved up her arms toward her shoulders. "Clare Mac," he said and leaned as though to kiss her.

She stepped back. "Why are you doing this?" she asked, biting off the words. "Why can't you just let everything be? I'm here today. Let today be. Okay?"

He studied her. "And tomorrow?"

"Tomorrow I go back to my life, and you have to find a way to go back to yours. Or to make a new one. But I'm here now. Isn't that enough? I came back."

His face completely changed. It went blank. *Blank with rage* was the phrase that went through her mind even as his arms caught her. He bent into his back, picked her up. He threw her overboard.

Her body plunged down into the moving ocean, which seemed to gulp her in, then to hold her as she fought for the surface. And even when she found it, the water moved around her, shifting and holding her, some giant live beast with Clare tiny in its palm. She felt the weight of it, the depth of it, the breadth. She was lost in it. Her will was subsumed in its bulk, in its roiling might and restlessness.

"Not funny," she screamed up to Riley. But she couldn't see him. He wasn't starboard. He was gone from her sight. Was he on the boat, or in the water?

Water came over her head. Her eyes burned with it, her nose. She felt all the airways in her head sear with the sudden rush of salt water. In that single breath, her anger at him turned to fear.

Coming up out of it, she craned to see him, but the water pressed in on her, tried to enter her again. Panic rose in her throat like bile. She was choking on herself as much as the seawater, suffocating. She opened her mouth to call out and only swallowed some of the rising water. It was in her nose and her eyes and her throat, though she still had the presence of mind to berate herself. She had come out here rashly. He was an injured man, an injured stranger. Riley was not all there, literally. And now where was she? Who even knew where she was?

Nobody knew.

The motor roared. She could hear it even over the terror that stormed in her ears. Through the blur of salt, she saw that Riley had the boat moving away from her, away away away. She tried to call out, but her voice was submerged in a sob. And then a whitecap broke over her head.

Even as she fought to keep her limbs moving, to anticipate the

movement of the water, and to keep her head in the air, her mind
cast about. The memory of the other time, the night they had gone
up on the ledge, lashed at her. She remembered the brawn of the
sea that night, and the water pulling at her and Riley holding on
to her, keeping her locked with one arm to himself. She thought
of how tiny Riley had seemed to her then, how insignificant he
was against what he had taken them into: this sea. She had kept
saying to herself, and even as she was saying it, she believed that
they would be the last words she ever spoke, "We were almost
home. We were almost home."

His face had been terrible to her then. He had done this to her,
she had thought. He had killed her, and he was terrible to her
suddenly. But he was all, then as now. He was her only hope. She
clung to the thought of him now, as she had clung to him with
her whole being years before.

"Riley," she called, and she felt how the water absorbed the
noise. She was in a trough, and even her voice couldn't rise above
it, free itself.

The boat kept moving. She caught glimpses of it when the
water swelled under her, shouldered her up.

"Riley," the word seemed to tear up out of her stomach. She
felt wrenched with the effort of reaching for him with only the
air in her lungs and the few frail cords of her larynx. What were
they to the vast voracity of this ocean? "Riley, please." She was in
the valley again, lost. Her voice puddled around her.

The next time the water lurched upward so that she could see
the boat, she had to strain to realize that she was actually seeing
it. It had grown small, the *Lily*. It looked like a child's toy, like
no kind of salvation at all. And Riley was merely a dot in it, like
the little plastic men that had climbed the masts on the ship models
her father used to help her put together. Riley looked small and
lifeless and unreal: inanimate. She could not even see his face

anymore. And, if he looked back, she was certain he could not see hers.

How could he find his way back to her, even if he relented? The waves were high, obliterating.

She batted at the water with her arms and legs, tried to move in the direction he had gone. But was that toward land or away? Who knew what he would do. She treaded water, confused. Then she thought, I have to go somewhere. She began to swim. She kicked off her shoes, her jeans, the cotton sweater she had buttoned over her tee shirt. But they turned out not to be the greatest weight on her. Fear was greater: wondering what lurked under the water; being lost under the sky; taking the last breath; knowing it was the last.

The ocean throbbed around her, and she concentrated on pulling herself along its surface. She concentrated on the water, its whims. When it swamped her from behind, she sputtered and gasped. "Okay," she told it. "Okay." Her voice was calm, as though it were a snarling dog she was feigning indifference toward, hoping she could get past it.

The cold was the worst. She knew she couldn't last long in it. Even in summer, the northern Atlantic didn't warm enough. Whenever she and Riley had gone swimming off the boat as kids, it had always been along sandbars. He had claimed the sun warmed the water there, but it always felt meanly cold to her. She had never swum for long, even with him stroking along behind her. "I feel like a swimming skeleton," she had told him once, her teeth clattering against each other. The cold had made her seem so aware of her bones.

And now was no different. She was aware of her anatomy, deeply aware of it, of the muscles sore with effort and the ember bones deep inside, of the circulating blood pressing behind her eyes. Her scars ached. She was aware, too, of her strength failing.

Still the ocean tossed her. It did seem alive around her. She thought she could hear it throbbing. It had a pulse. She heard it in her ears, felt it along her spine. And then she saw why. It was the boat's engine. It was Riley coming back.

The *Lily* loomed over her, cast its bulk between her eyes and the sun. She squinted up. The water washed over her again. She breathed through it, coughed.

"Take my hand," Riley said. She could see him, dark against the sun. He leaned down to her.

She had no choice but to reach for him. His hand closed around hers, knotted itself like rope. He hauled her in, held out a blanket, and wrapped her in it. He pulled her tight against him.

"You could have killed me," she said, trying to wrench free of his hold. But she was bound in the blanket, in his arms.

"I would never let anything happen to you, Clare." His voice was calm with an undercurrent of emotion.

She tried to flail free of him with all her remaining strength, sobbing and doing the only thing she could to hurt him: She bit at his shoulder. It was hard as marble.

He sat down, fell really, and pulled her with him, holding her arms against her rib cage. The boat tossed unpredictably, and it took Clare a minute to realize that Riley too was rocking her back and forth. He murmured into her sodden hair where it clung to her temple. He kissed her forehead, his lips moving in whatever words he was saying more to himself than to her.

She fought to breathe through her tears. It was as though the Atlantic had entered her, and the waves of her fear and anguish and relief kept coming over her, engulfing her, relentlessly, relentlessly.

"Forgive me," he said finally. His voice was utterly calm. "I had to make you understand." His voice made to caress her as his hands were. "But I wasn't thinking. I wasn't using my head. It was just like my body was in charge. I just needed for you to understand. Nobody understands, Clare."

She went limp against him, gave up, and listened through her tears. It was not a choice she made, listening to him. It was simply that there was not much left in her with which to continue fighting.

"Do you?" he asked. "Do you understand?"

Her head was pressed into the hollow of his neck. She shook it. No. How could she? She might have died. Easily, she might have died. He could not have known that he was not hurling her to her death. He could not have known what the sea would do, could not have unfailingly known that he would find her again in the midst of the roiling waves. He could not have known that she would remember how to keep herself afloat in the midst of her panic.

"Don't you understand? Oh, Clare. I'm sorry. I am sorry. But it's the same thing you're doing to me."

"I didn't do anything to you," she said into his shirt, which was as wet now as she was. "I was a million miles away when you had your accident, and I only came back because I wanted to help. I came back to help you." She hoped the acid of her feeling would burn into him, scorch him with the shame of his actions.

"You said you had to leave," he defended himself. "You said you had to leave tomorrow." As if that were accusation enough to have consigned her to the waters, to drowning.

She fought him one more time. It surprised him, and he lost his grip. She fell back on the floor hard. But she could see his eyes from there, could make him see hers. "I do have to leave," she said. Defiance sputtered in her, fought like a fire to get enough air. Physically spent as she was, she defied him with her eyes.

"Don't," he said, leaning in and taking her by the shoulders, which she had freed from the blanket. His grip seemed to sink into her muscle. His fingers seemed to penetrate her flesh.

"You're hurting me."

"You're hurting me," he echoed. "Don't you think I know there's something wrong with me? Don't you think I know that, Clare?"

She looked at him, couldn't find words. She could see the pain in his eyes. No, it was panic. His features twitched with it. He was terrified and trapped.

He said, "Everybody tells me I'm missing something from my life. Don't you think I know that? Don't you think I know I've got a hole blown in my head as big as this ocean?" He stood suddenly, jerkily as a reflex. In one step, he was up on the side of the boat, balancing. He yelled, "I know that." He was shaking hard, almost convulsively.

Standing up, she put her hand on his belt. It went through her mind that she didn't know if she wanted to push him over the side or bring him back down to safety. But she finally looped her fingers around the military weave of the belt. Her voice said, "Come down, Riley. Come down."

His body swayed on the narrow side of the boat, and she did not know which way he would go. She could not predict. She did not know if she cared really, except for what it meant to her own safety. He seemed so lost, whether he fell or not. What did it matter? His life was a hell of confusion, of danger that lay within himself as much as it lay without. His life had become, without his bidding it, a place with no guideposts. He couldn't look to the stars to find his way. He couldn't place himself by the slight slant of the sun at high noon. The moon in its phases was no help to him, nor was the direction of the wind. He was lost.

Standing there, linked to him by the barest hold, Clare realized that she had been on the brink of that abyss within herself. She did understand his wanting out of it. She did understand his wanting rescue from it, any rescue. Wanting rescue so desperately that anything seemed justified.

"Riley," she said again, softly. "Come down, okay? I understand. I do."

After a minute, he turned his head and looked down at her. His eyes were filled with tears. She was relieved to see the tears, to see in him someone she recognized. Someone she could help. "Come here, Riley," she said.

He came down into her arms. She held him. His arms were loose at his sides, but as she heard sobs start to heave through him, he put his arms around her, held on tightly. His body gave off a heat, almost a scent of anguish. He smoldered in her embrace.

"I just wanted you to understand," he said after a few minutes. "I just needed you to *get* it."

"Okay," she murmured. "Okay."

"Clare, it's like somebody threw me overboard. It's like somebody somewhere just pitched me overboard and left me. Bye. Stranded. And you're all I can see. You're the only hope I have. You're the only thing I know that I love. And that's the only thing I trust in the world. The only thing. Loving you."

"Riley," she said.

"I trust you," he said, holding her tightly. "You're the only one. It makes no sense to anybody else, apparently. But it's the one thing that does make sense to me."

"Okay."

"How can I love you so much, and you not feel anything? You have to feel something." His arms tightened around her. "You have to, Clare Mac."

She hesitated, but responded finally to the need in his eyes and to something old in herself that was moved by it. "I do feel something for you, Riley. But . . ."

"No 'buts,' Clare," he said, running his fingers along the line of her chin. "Please. We'll deal with 'buts' when we get to them."

"We've already gotten to them, Riley." It was barely a whisper though.

He brought his lips to hers, silencing her. He moved slowly, as though he questioned whether he should. When he touched her, the pads of his lips were soft as a child's and so warm to her after having been caught in the cold water of the ocean. His warmth seemed to enter her through his kiss, through his searching mouth.

She accepted the kiss. Maybe because the warmth of him so soothed her, radiating from the kiss and soaking through her, deep into her. Or maybe she was as lost as he was, as far out to sea in her emotions. Before Riley had thrown her into the northern Atlantic waters, before she had come back to Ledgemere to see him, before she had even received his wife's postcard, she had been as unmoored as he was. She too had somehow lost her bearings.

They stood there in the bright sun in a tiny tossing boat. They could not see land from where they were. They could not smell it. All they knew was what was within reach: these arms, these eyes, these lips moving hard together, this breath drawn from each other. This moment. This rescue.

Clare pulled away first. She turned, gripped the sides of the boat, steadied herself. Riley's shadow fell down over the side, next to hers, both of them floating like oil in the uneasy water. She felt as disembodied as her shadow. Finally, she looked over at him. "I have to . . ." she tried. "I can't . . ."

"Shhhh," he said. "Thank you." He reached to brush the outside of his fingers against her cheek.

"Thank you," she said, and meant it. Air seemed to move again into her lungs. Feeling came back into her arms, her legs. It pounded in her head, at both temples. Clare came back to herself, to her reality. He let her come back.

"You're shivering," he said.

"Of course I am. I'm wet to the quick, and I have no pants or shoes. Some madman threw me overboard." She was teasing. She was serious.

He winced and grinned. "I'm sorry, Clare."

"I'm sorry too," she said, though she couldn't have said for what she was sorry or to whom she owed the apology. For now, her urge to analyze everything had been doused. She felt like a being of blood and flesh and hunger and pain. Nothing more.

ᘓᘚ

Riley steered toward one of the outlying islands, and when he had pulled up close to the scarred wood of the dock, he tied on the rubber-ball fenders and secured the *Lily* with quick loops of soft line. "Don't go anywhere," he told her out of one side of his mouth, as he jumped over the side.

"Funny," she mumbled after him, cowering in the shade of the *Lily*'s cap, wearing only her damp tee shirt and cotton panties, along with a glaringly yellow rain slicker and some mildewed rubber boots that Maggie had stowed away in the glory hole maybe a decade ago. The slicker smelled like rotten fish, and Clare couldn't stop thinking about the fact that her favorite Nike hikers were lost at sea, along with her Levi's. Fish food.

She thought of a codfish nudging her Nikes, and the image made her giggle. She was giddy with relief. She was numb with it and loose with it: unhinged. She *was* relief.

Riley, too, was almost tipsy with the aftermath of averted disaster. He thought her predicament now was hilarious. Even as he walked away from her toward the little store on the landing, she could see the grin on his face. It was in the cocked angle of his shoulders, in the particular rolling swagger of his step.

As she waited, Clare could see people sitting on the railing farther up the dock, tilting their heads to lick ice cre⹁ ᾽ from cones. There were children jumping off the pilings into t high tide of the harbor. Their screams rose up out of them like rᴄ ased pressure.

The *Lily* snuffled at the mooring, seemingly as impatient as Clare herself. Finally she saw Riley coming toward her with an armload of brown bags. He yelled a teasing good-bye to someone over his shoulder. "That'll be the day," he said. He seemed drunk even to Clare, and she knew better.

"What took you so long?" she asked when he landed in the *Lily* and tossed a bag at her. She pulled out a horribly pink sweatshirt, size XXL. It had a lobster printed on it that clanged red all over the front.

"Didn't they have any other color?" she asked him.

"You like pink," he said.

"On peonies and sunsets," she said, pulling the shirt over her head. "Not on me."

The sweatpants were gray, at least, though they too had a lobster plastered on the back pocket. "Lovely," she quipped as she pulled them up. They too were a size XXL. She stood there with the folds of clothes falling around her, and Riley began to laugh. "Who let the air out of you?" he teased.

"That would be you," she said. "That would definitely be you, my friend."

The *Lily* coughed back to full steam, and Riley headed her to the east. Clare rummaged through the bag of food: french fries, fried clam rolls, cole slaw. The smell of the fried clams was overpowering. After the long-ago cappuccino and the plunge in the rough ocean and the retreat from precipitous emotion, Clare was ravenous.

"Save some for me," Riley said, as he saw her picking out the clams, eating them from her palm like popcorn.

He pulled into a sheltered harbor between two little islands,

Randalls and Little Berry. They seemed to be covered only with a burnished vegetation, growing low to the ground. "Best strawberries in the world," he bragged. "Sweet."

Dropping anchor in the calmer water, Riley knelt down on the deck next to Clare and reached for the food. He settled cross-legged, and they ate in silence for a while, with only the pestering *scree* of the gulls. It was a relief, she thought, this moment that they'd come to. It was the kind of moment that you had to earn by endurance. It was what was waiting on the other side of terrible.

After a while, Riley leaned against the side and stretched his legs out. He sighed. "Oh, well, out here it doesn't much matter," he said.

"What doesn't matter?"

"The rest of the world."

She tipped her head back and looked at the sky and almost wished that it were true. But it wasn't. Not for her. She knew she had trespassed on her husband's trust today, was in danger of worse. She knew she felt something on this open water, something that seemed an island of emotion, something set apart from the world where she lived every day. But it couldn't be set apart. If it didn't seem to matter at this moment, in this slant of light, it would later. She knew that. "It does matter," she said.

"I know," he said solemnly.

He reached for her hand where it lay on the deck between them. With a finger, he stroked the ridge of her knuckles. They were both quiet. The boat rolled softly.

"Did they tell you that I cry when I see the little girls?" he asked after a long silence.

She looked at him. This was a new direction. This was somewhere she could follow. She shook her head. Nobody had told her how he had reacted to his family.

He exhaled loudly. "I know the doctors aren't lying, Clare. I know Laurie's not. But I can't deal with them anymore. Laurie keeps badgering me, like I'm just going to pick up where she says I left off. Like she's been keeping my place in a book. Only I don't remember the rest of the story, what's already happened." His gaze moved back and forth across the horizon, as though he were half-waiting for something to appear. "And I really don't feel anything for her," he said. "Nothing."

"You don't remember her at all?"

"Sure, I remember her. I started kindergarten with her. I remember this one time—clear as a snapshot. She fell off the monkey bars in second grade, and she was really crying and a green snot bubble came out her nose."

"Oh, Riley," Clare admonished him.

"No, I'm serious. I see it clear as that gull." He pointed to a pristinely white gull that tipped in the wind just over the boat, opened its beak, closed it, opened it again, squawked. "And I remember that she made great cookies for the bake sales, and that I danced with her once at the prom because she had brought her uncle as her date. The guys called her Thunder Thighs."

"You don't remember falling in love with her?"

He leveled his gaze at her. His voice was hard, "Did I fall in love with her?"

"Didn't you?"

"I can't even imagine it." The words were harsh, might have seemed mean-spirited had they not been softened by regret. It wasn't a willful statement. Just an honest one.

She keened out a breath. She meant it sympathetically. What could she say?

Riley's face flushed. When he spoke again, it was with a coiled tone. "It's so damned frustrating. But it's just like somebody's sliced away the knot." He gestured in the air, a fierce slash. "It's like whatever attached me to them is gone. I'm just adrift out here."

She waited.

"And there's only you. Like some kind of beacon."

"I can't pretend to understand," she told him. "It must be scary though."

He looked at her, and fear was the very blue of his irises. Stark. His gaze shifted back to the sky and the wheeling birds. "They're beautiful kids," he said. "Have you seen them?" He turned again to see her answer.

She nodded.

He said, "That older one, she looks just like my mom. Hell, I know she belongs to me. But I look at her, and all I see is how much she wants from me. How much she expects. I'm her Daddy." He said the word with gravity and then shook his head as if to free himself of the weight of it. His eyes were wet. "But I look at her, and I don't even know who she is. I don't know her. I don't know what kind of day it was when she was born, or maybe it was nighttime. I don't know when she started walking, or what she said when she started talking. I don't know what she likes to eat, and if she can stay in the lines when she colors. I don't know if she can tie her own shoes. She's this little stranger."

Clare squeezed his hand, slid over closer to him.

"The poor little kid," he said mournfully. "Laurie brought her out one day, and she wanted to go make a fairy house in the woods. And I wouldn't do it. Because I was sure I must have done that with her umpteen times. But I don't remember it once. I didn't want to show her, prove to her that I didn't remember anything about her." He looked at Clare through a glaze of tears.

She brought his hand onto her lap, held it in both of hers. "You'll remember," she said.

"How do you know?" he said, as though he really did want to know where her certainty came from. There was a hard demand in his tone.

And she couldn't answer that. She didn't know.

He said, "You're going to stay, aren't you? You won't leave me alone, Clare?" He wasn't begging. There was nothing weak in the question. He was being straightforward about what he wanted, what he felt he needed.

She had to look away from him. "Riley," she said. Her spine tensed.

"Don't panic," he said. He touched her chin, drew her gaze back to his. "Don't panic, okay. Explain to me. I'll listen."

"His name is Michael," she said.

"Your husband?"

She nodded. "Seven years."

"And you love him?"

"Of course."

"Don't get testy, Clare. Sometimes it's not about love."

"I love him," she said. "Very much."

Riley absorbed this. "Okay," he said. He sat up straighter, turned so he could face her. "Where is he now?"

She looked at her hands.

"I mean, why are you here and he's somewhere else?"

"He has obligations," she said, trying to hold her eyes steady in his.

"Other than you?" Riley asked, unblinkingly.

"His mother is sick." Clare could hear spikes of defense in her voice. She struggled against the feeling that she had to justify her choices, Michael's.

Riley said, "She needed him? And he's a good guy, so he went?"

Clare nodded.

"So why aren't you there helping him help her?"

Clare laughed at his interrogation, but something—anger or maybe her own persistent questions in this vein—ticked at the back of her throat. "Because I'm here helping you," she said, trying to keep her voice even.

"Helping me?" He smiled. "So it's more important to you to help me than to help him help her?"

"That's not fair." She laughed because she didn't know how else to react. "Enough," she protested. "Enough."

"You're right," he said. "It is enough. I know everything I need to know." He got up then and walked to the helm, bent to start the engine, and turned toward Ledgemere Island, toward home.

Clare had to walk up the hill from the landing and through the village in her size XXL clothes and the mildewed rubber boots. The boots made, alternately, a sucking and a slapping sound. A few tourists gave her a second glance, but discreetly. Ledgemere was an artists' colony, after all, and its eccentrics were part of its character. No one would want to stare openly and chance scaring any bit of the local color under the nearest cover.

When Clare came into the lobby, Maggie said, "Are those my old rubbers?"

"Yep." Clare let the screen door snap closed behind her.

Maggie shook her head. "What did he do now?"

"Long story."

"From the looks of you, I'll bet it is a long story." She pitched her head back and laughed so hard that Clare thought it would rattle the average ninety-year-old frame right out of its sockets. But not Maggie's.

Clare had her hand on the staircase railing, anxious to get into a hot bath. She had lifted her foot to make the first step, when Maggie stopped her hysterics long enough to say, "You're probably in no mood for it, but you've got company."

"Company?" Clare's mind shuffled through the possibilities. Her hopes rose highest to the possibility of Michael. Maybe he had torn himself out of the chaos and decided he needed to get away. Maybe . . .

"It's Laurie, poor thing," Maggie said. "I've got her out in the kitchen stemming strawberries for me. Keeps her mind occupied, you know." The old woman came closer to Clare and shook her by the wrist. She whispered, "We didn't know where the two of you had got off to for so long. Who knew?" She raised an eyebrow.

Clare closed both her eyes and blew out a long breath.

"Where is he now?" Maggie asked.

"Down at the landing talking to the guys, last I saw."

"Good," Maggie said. "I'll set you two girls up with some tea, and you'll have a nice chat."

᎒᎒

Clare gave up the idea of a long soak in the clawfoot tub, and instead pulled on some leggings and one of Michael's old denim shirts. She usually found the shirt comforting in its familiarity. She liked the idea of it having touched his skin as it now touched hers. But as she buttoned it up, she flushed with a sudden anger. Was she supposed to make do with only his cast-off clothes all the time?

Was she supposed to just go on living without the warmth of him next to her? She stripped the shirt up over her head and dug a cotton tunic out of her bag. She pulled it roughly over her head.

Bending at the waist, she shook her stiff hair, tried to shake some life back into it. She could feel the dried salt encrusted along each strand. Oh, well. There was no time to deal with it now. The sooner she went downstairs, the sooner she could retreat back up here, close her door on it all, lock it.

It annoyed her that Laurie had come: checking up, it felt like. The fact of her annoyance shamed Clare, but it was as though Riley had cast her out of reality today when he had thrown her into the Atlantic. It was as though when he had reached to bring her back aboard, he had brought her back into his reality, onto his skewed plane of existence. Now, she had her footing there, and she did not know why, but it made her feel off balance to have to face Laurie.

Betrayal, she thought. It felt like a betrayal of Riley to plumb his psyche and then report back to his wife. She had not been on a reconnaissance mission today, out there on the *Lily*. She had not been there on Laurie's behalf. She had been there because she wanted to be. Something in Riley's pain nudged close to her own. Something in his plaint belonged as much to her. It had been a comfort to her, holding his hand. It was a reciprocal act. He had been holding her hand too, hadn't he?

Clare's boiled-wool clogs scuffed loudly on the hardwood floors of the dining room, and everyone looked up to see her crossing the floor to the table where Riley's wife sat. Laurie was looking out the window toward the little house where Riley now lived as a bachelor. She was the only one in the vast echoing dining hall who didn't turn to watch Clare's progress. Her sister Kim, standing by the kitchen door with the hostess, never took her eyes off Clare. It was a penetrating stare, and Clare felt it to the bone.

"Laurie?" Clare said, pausing across the table from Riley's wife.

The woman looked up at her. She ran her hands over her face, as though to wipe away what she had been thinking. She clawed the hair back off her face. "Sorry," she said, still looking miserable despite her efforts.

"It's okay," Clare said. "Maybe I should give you some time."

"No, sit down."

"Did you bring the girls?" Clare said.

"Oh, no. They're with their grammy." She tipped her head as if to rest it on her own shoulder. "It's easier for them not to see him like this." Tears welled up in her eyes. She bit her lip, fought herself.

Clare looked away from the other woman's pain, looked out the window. She saw what Laurie had seen. Riley was painting his lobster buoys. Wearing his rubber apron and the high boots, he seemed lost in his task, painting elaborate designs with his teal and yellow paint. The ones he had finished hung over the cottage. It might have been decorated for some Mexican festival.

Laurie said, "I'm sorry. I'm usually stronger about it. But this has opened it all back up again, coming over. Seeing him. Seeing him look so happy . . . as though nothing had happened."

Clare said, "I'm so sorry, Laurie."

Tears rolled down Laurie's face. "He used to hold my hand," she said, "every night when we were falling asleep." She paused, looked out the window at him. "Sometimes I miss it so much. Just his hand."

After a minute, Laurie, rubbed the tears off her cheeks. "What did he say . . . when he saw you?"

"He thought my hair was shorter." Clare knew she was not helping Laurie, was not answering the questions that Laurie couldn't even ask. "It didn't work, Laurie," she admitted. "I don't think you can count on him just snapping out of it one day."

"Now you're the expert," Laurie said bitterly.

Clare didn't acknowledge the tone. "It's not that," she said. "It's just that he *wants* to be better. He *wants* to remember. He really *can't*. He can see that Mandy belongs to him, but he can't feel it. That's gnawing on him."

"He told you that?"

Clare nodded. She could see pain come down across Laurie's face, followed by a curtain of blankness.

"Of course, he told you," Laurie said flatly. "I'll live his crazy life with him for ten years. I'll have two babies for him. I'll get up at four in the dark morning until eternity comes to see that he's got something hot in his thermos when he's out pulling his traps. But he can't open his mouth and tell me what he's feeling. He has to tell you." She couldn't quite lift her accusation to meet Clare's eyes. "He hasn't seen you in seventeen years."

"I know it's hard for you to hear," Clare said. "But sometimes it's easier to tell someone less involved. Sometimes you need to tell someone who doesn't care as much. It's easier. There's not as much at stake."

"And you know this from your own hard life?" Laurie cracked.

"Yes," Clare told her, "I do."

Clare sat in the darkness on the front porch, waiting her turn. A teenage girl was on the sole pay phone, her hand cupped around the mouthpiece, whispering love to someone faraway. For maybe an hour—she lost track of how long it was—Clare was content to suspend herself in the black night, to tilt her head to the stars and let the murmur of the girl's love drift by like some faint medieval harp music. Clare had done her duty to Laurie, had even walked her down to the last Sky Hill ferry. Then she had pleaded exhaustion to Riley and had gone upstairs to a long hot soak in the clawfoot tub. She had steeped herself in solitude.

The constellations were bright again tonight, she noticed. She picked out Virgo, and also Sagittarius and Scorpius suspended in a filmy swath of the Milky Way. There was Arcturus at the tip of Boötes. Polaris must be behind her. She told herself that later, before going up to bed, she should look for it and for Sirius, too, the eye of the dog.

It had been a long time since she had studied the stars, delved into the cosmic mysteries. After what had happened that last night with Riley, it had been her obsession. But that had passed with the worst of her pain, and she was surprised now that so much was still with her, so much of what she had read in that old field guide. It was like looking back into her past life, into that past season of mourning, to look up and read the skies, recognize the constellations and their brightest stars. And it was, literally, a way of seeing backward. Gazing into the night sky was an act of looking back into the far reaches of time. It had taken the light of the stars millions, sometimes billions of years to reach her eye. She was looking at the past.

Michael, she thought with a jolt, struggling to reorient herself. What time had it gotten to be? Would it be too late to call?

The rocking chair creaked as Clare leaned forward onto her knees. It sounded like impatience itself. The girl on the phone swiveled a wary glance over her shoulder, then hunched back into her conversation. She giggled. She could not bear to give up the phone.

Clare stood and walked down the steps onto the gravel road. There used to be another phone outside the general store. Even from the top of the hill, she could see that the store was closed up and dark. There not even a night-light burning inside. When she stepped up on the porch and found the phone, she had to punch in the numbers by touch. The receiver was cool in her hand, though it still smelled of somebody else's perfume, of the accretion of many people's breaths. Standing there with the buzz sounding on the other end—once, twice, again, again, again—Clare felt outside herself, a stranger waiting for a familiar voice to answer her call.

Del picked up after six rings. She was out of breath and irritated. Her greeting was almost preemptive. She didn't have time for this.

"Hi, Del. It's Clare calling," Clare said into the mouthpiece, feeling disconnected to the other end of the line, but keeping her voice low anyway. She feared it would carry up and down the hushed roads of the island village.

"Oh, Clare," Del huffed. Then she hesitated.

Clare hurried in. "Is Michael there?"

"He is," Del said. "But he's not available right now."

Not available? Clare was calling her husband for the first time in three days, and he wasn't available? She could hear his voice in the background, a muffled baritone. He was obviously right there. What was he doing that he couldn't speak to her? Was his mother hurt? Had he himself been injured on one of the ladders? What did Del mean by telling Clare simply, cryptically, that he was unavailable? If there was a reason he couldn't speak with her, if the timing was bad, she at least deserved to know why. She wasn't an anonymous phone solicitor. She was his wife.

"I'm calling from a pay phone," Clare told Del, and she hated the humiliation of trying to justify why she needed Michael now, when he was right there and she could hear that he was right there. She asked so little of him, of her in-laws. She asked almost nothing. She knew they had almost nothing left to give.

"Clare?" Michael's voice was as harried as Del's when he came on the line. "We're giving Mommy Belle a shower. Is everything okay?"

She choked up a yes, got it past the lump that had swelled into her throat. Something burned behind her eyes. Yes, everything was okay, she said. She was just calling to catch up with him.

The voices of the two women rose in the background. Belle's voice shrieked. Del's beat like a military drum, fighting to conjure order out of the chaos of a battle.

Michael's answer was too long in coming. "That's good," he said.

"Okay," she said. "Are you all right?"

"Fine," he said. "Sure." Then, he barked a warning into the room, "She's slipping."

"Oh, Michael," Clare said.

"Christ," he muttered. Then he asked briskly, "Are you home yet?"

He hadn't even called to see. She might be anywhere, and he wouldn't know. And even as she thought it, she rebuked herself. Why should Michael lift his head out of hell to wonder after her whereabouts?

"I'm still in Maine," she said.

"That's good. . . . I've got to go, Clare. I'm sorry. You'd think we were torturing her instead of giving her a nice shower to cool her off. She's got a lot of strength."

"Good luck," Clare whispered. "Take care of yourself. Bye."

"Take care of yourself," he echoed, but she was already arcing the phone back into its cradle. His voice came from far away, across all the distance between them, faded away, faded to black. And as she turned, and the constellations reeled around her, she remembered that other theory, the one about the big bang. If it were true, it meant that the universe was still expanding, rippling out from one first huge explosion. It meant that every distant object was slowly and inexorably growing more distant, moving farther and farther away.

—☊☋—

Her footsteps were quiet on the road going home. Behind some windows there was lantern light, and it made the rooms seem filled with honey. She saw people reading. She saw families with their heads bent in unison over a game board. From somewhere up the hill, from a house hidden in the trees, she heard guitar music. Several women were singing a Joni Mitchell song with great feeling. *Skate away . . .*

The light was off in Riley's upstairs room. She crossed the lawn of the hotel and stood looking up at it. The chill from the damp grass soaked through her clogs and into the soles of her feet. She snugged the sweater tight around her and thought: summer in Maine. There was a fire on the hearth in the hotel lobby, just waiting for her. There was the old beloved copy of Gerard Manley Hopkins's poetry on the shelf; she had checked on that last night. She should hurry inside where it was warm, tuck her legs under her, and read about the wimpling wing of a windhover. She should.

Instead she went to the edge of the road and scuffled with the toe of her shoe until she dislodged a shard of seashell. It was as fine as an eggshell between her fingers. She went back below Riley's window, aimed, and pitched.

She heard him stir. His head came out the window. "Is that you?" he whispered from the husky depths of his diaphragm.

"Who else throws shells at you?"

"Come up," he said.

"Take a walk with me."

He disappeared from the window and reappeared minutes later, coming around the corner and out of the shadow of the little building. He said, "I can see your breath."

"It's not that cold."

Riley fell in beside her. They walked out of town, out toward where the road broke from the trees into paths that ran among the sea grass and down onto the rocks. When they emerged out of the night shade of the firs, Clare gasped at the sky. Here, beyond the weak lights of the village, it was even brighter. She could see in it the trailing wisps of light from the Milky Way.

They seemed as though someone had brushed the intensity of the stars, painted them out into mere veils of luminence. Riley put his hands on her shoulders from behind, and they stopped and absorbed it.

After they had stood in silence for a while, Riley started to climb over the boulders toward the water. She stayed behind. She watched his legs stretch from one foothold to another, watched the way he held his arms outstretched, balancing his weight. He was a shadow against the bright sky.

"Aren't you coming?" he asked, turning to wait for her. He held out his hand.

"Let's don't go any farther," she said. She still didn't trust the waves.

He came back toward her, sat down on a rock, and made space for her to sit next to him. She sat, and when he put his arm around her, she let it stay. The silence and their togetherness here felt safe to her, not mined with expectations. Riley was, had always been, her friend. Her aunt had said, "You trail him around like a security blanket." Oh well, she could admit it now: She had needed a security blanket that summer.

After some minutes, Riley brushed the skin of her forehead with a faint touch of his lips. Her throat tightened around her rebuke but then softened again as he caught himself, sighed, laid his cheek on the crown of her head. He grew quiet again, so quiet that when his voice rose unexpectedly out of the night, she felt it run through her nerves. He said, "It's the only time I remember making love, Clare. That night, out there ... the night of the eclipse."

She sat motionless, waiting for him to go on, hoping he wouldn't, waiting for him ...

"I must've done it hundreds of times since then, Clare: made love." He had trouble even saying it. The words were awkward in his mouth. "I must've. Hell, I made two babies." His voice trailed off, and she thought he was finished. Then he said, "But that's the only time I remember. That might as well be the only time I've been so close to anyone ever. It's the only time I have."

He lapsed back into a stillness that stretched on, and because she didn't know what to say to him, she stayed still too. She tried to imagine what it would be like for her—if that was all she had ever known of love, if that night when he had taken her out on his new boat had been her only memory of coming close, of entering into another person's presence.

They had chosen the night because of the lunar eclipse. That was their excuse for going out alone on the water. And neither of them ever spoke out loud of the possibility of going so deeply into each other, though Clare had known that part of her wanted to go that deeply into him, into herself, into life. Death was too much a governor for her. She wanted to live.

It had happened at the end of the summer. She was supposed to leave the next week. Her parents had no choice but to let her come home finally, even though her mother was lingering, still suffering, and surely they didn't want to have kept their daughter away for all but the bitterest end. But school was about to start, and even her father admitted Clare would be better off in her own orbit, buffered by routine. It would be different than the summertime, when she would have had nothing to occupy her days, nothing but the long vigil of her mother's illness.

So on that night of the moon's eclipse, Clare knew she was leaving Maine soon, leaving Riley. She knew that she was going home to watch her mother die. Riley had known too, though they had rarely spoken of why Clare was in Sky Hill, why it was so difficult for her to think of going home, why she wanted as much to stay as to go. But he was as aware of her reality as she was, she always thought. There was something about the tight way he held her sometimes, something that had nothing to do with passion. He tried in his way to protect her from what waited for her.

Getting the boat a month early was supposed to be her going-away present. He had taken her out to Ledgemere for another weekend with Maggie and his grandmother chaperoning, however ineffectually. He and Clare both knew it would be their last on the island. After some furtive behavior at the landing, he had loaded her into the tender, started rowing. And there, anchored in the harbor, was his new boat. She was afraid to look at it.

For weeks, he had promised her, "Clare Mac, I'm going to name it after you." Now, she was mortified to think that Riley Brackett had gone and done it: He would be plying the waters of St. George's Bay in a boat that heralded his love for her. The *Clare Mac*. It was a possibility too flamboyant for the midwesterner in her. It was too much a black-and-white, tangible symbol of what it was they secretly felt for one another, what they believed to be love—that buzzing in the ears, that rustling of blood, that burst of light behind the eyelids. Naming his boat after her seemed like too great an opportunity for revealing their foolishness. Even then, she did have a sober inkling: if not that it was truly foolish of them to make promises to one another, at least that it would be perceived as foolishness.

So from her place in the little tender in which she faced Riley as he rowed, she had to make herself look over his shoulder. She had to make herself look past him and toward his new fishing boat. It was freshly painted white and yellow. And the black letters on its stern were still wet.

"I told you," he said, his face creasing into mirth. "I named her after you." Mischief beamed off him.

The boat was the *After You*. He roared with laughter.

Relieved giggles had bubbled out of Clare like champagne. She saw how proudly his eyes reached along the boat's solid lines. He

helped her aboard and talked feverishly about how much money
he could make between now and when the season froze over and
made the work too miserable. "Mornings *before* school," he em-
phasized. "Weekends."

They had a deal about school. They had a deal in general. No,
they had promises. When Clare thought about it later, she had
always supposed that Riley had conspired with her in a fantasy
life meant to distract her from her real life, from losing her
mother. They schemed about marriage and about an island cottage
where she would can tomatoes from their garden and paint sea-
scapes. Her name would be on a shingle, and once a week she
would open her studio, and Ledgemere tourists would come and
buy her work and praise her.

It was unrealistic on her part. Though she admired art, Clare
had never painted until she bought watercolors and paper on her
first visit to Ledgemere. She showed no sign of talent from the
beginning, and even by summer's end she was no more accomplished. Her colors were muddy on the tablet. But a fantasy was
a fantasy. It was painted of different colors altogether.

Riley's part of the promise was more realistic. The waters off
Ledgemere were ripe with lobsters. "Like picking strawberries in
July," he boasted. He had lobstered with his father for so many
years that he knew the habits of the crustaceans, knew how to
read their migrations, how to shift his traps away from the best
spots at the right time, just when the population began to ebb.
Riley could uphold his part of the life they planned together. So
to him it was not so much fantasy as fact-in-waiting.

She couldn't remember if it had been more than necessary fantasy to her on that night he first took her aboard the *After You.*
She couldn't remember if it was ever real to her that they might
spend their lives together on that island off the coast of Maine.
After what happened, it didn't matter.

Still, sitting here with him on the rocky ledges of what had been "their" island, she discovered that, try as she had, she had not forgotten what they had once been to each other. She had not forgotten what might have been. These past days, she had been reminded of the colors she had seen in the world through his eyes, the amplification of birdsong when her head had rested in his lap, the way nothing, nothing ever, had been as soft as the skin under his cotton shirts. The memories were all still there, deep in space, lapsing farther away in all these intervening years. But the light of them did still reach her. She did remember.

And those sensual echoes drew her back to that night, all the way back, far past where she had ever allowed herself to go. Now, for once, she allowed herself the experience of her memories: the terror, the glory. All of it.

On the night of the lunar eclipse, their last together, they had taken a picnic supper out on the boat. It had been a calm day. Earlier they had hiked around the island, picking raspberries as they went, and when they had emerged from the trees onto the cliffs that faced the open sea, they had seen the ocean stretched like a deeper blue mirror of the sky. "A blue day," she had called it. They had lain in one of the meadows and gathered long stems of daisies and red clover, which she had made into a necklace. She had worked absorbedly, splitting the green flesh of the stalk and needling another through it, weaving on one link, then another, until it was a lush loop.

"He loves me; he loves me not," Riley kept track of each blossom as she worked.

"You have to tear them up to do that," she said. "Strip them of their petals."

"You can do it this way too," he said. "And this way you make sure it turns out right."

"He loves me," he said, as she worked in a daisy. "Stop there." She looked up at him.

"He loves you," he said.

Later, dressing for him, she had worn the daisy chain as an adornment to her pale yellow tee shirt and her cutoffs. Helping her onto his boat, Riley said the white of the flowers showed off her tan. He had steered the *After You* "toward France," as he put it, and then had cast anchor when they were out of sight of anything or anyone. The late sun on their faces was amber, and Clare was nervous and talked too much. She told him how the sap from ancient trees caught things, preserved them forever in a bubble the same color as this light. "Good," he said. "I don't want it ever to change."

As the sun dropped lower, they ate Maggie's biscuits with the cold meats and the sliced tomatoes. It was a slow agony of expectation, waiting for one another. She was so aware of him—the rhythm of his breath, the brightness of his earlobe, the wet gleam of his lower lip. Riley lay beside her, propped on his elbows, and she fed him raspberries from the basket and broken bits of a Hershey bar. "Melt the chocolate on your tongue," she had instructed him, "and then eat the raspberries."

"Isn't that good?" she asked him. She would say anything, she thought, to stave off the moment, to make it come at last. She felt that she was knitted together only by wild sensation, felt that she might dissolve and rise in the atmosphere, might hang like a haze of cloud burning in the last late sun.

Riley saved her. He had sat up suddenly and pulled her snugly against him. He had kissed her then, long and lovingly. But even his tenderness couldn't disguise the urgency he felt, the urgency that was even then quickening in her too, building.

Deep down, she had known this was what they had come for.

He must have known as well. They had called it the christening of the boat. They had talked of the wine he had pilfered from Maggie's hotel cellar. They had set the time for the eclipse of the moon. But they had known, though it was never spoken, that they were there to be together, to make promises they couldn't speak, to seal them. They had come to love each other.

The chocolate was sweet on his tongue, and the berries tart. Below both was the warm sour tinge of the wine, and below everything else—and they kissed so long without breathing that she tasted it even in that first kiss of utter release—there was the seawater sharpness of Riley himself. Kissing him was like the awful thrill of swallowing raw oysters. They had kissed before, kissed deeply. But she had not gone so far into him before, had not felt him penetrate to such depth in her. She knew that she would let him in, that she would open herself and let him blow through her like fresh wind, let him blow away what waited for her at home, let him promise in the only way he could that would bind them forever. The promise would be cast in the last amber light of sunset on the ocean.

He laid her down on the blanket that had been their picnic table, and she watched his hand move over the places of her body that she had kept to herself until this moment. His lips were on her breasts, on the hollow of her stomach. And then she saw him raise his eyes to her, his heart seemingly broken into pieces in his very gaze, and rise above her, cover her, envelope her even as she took him in. She closed her eyes.

The moon startled her when she came back to herself. It had shouldered up out of the ocean, huge and orange. Riley, when he raised himself, turned to a shadow as he moved between her and the moon, where it hung low, still absorbing the sun from the other side of the world. "Clare," he said later, "I saw the moon rise in your eyes."

It rose through the hours of the evening, growing smaller and higher, growing more pale. Then the shadow of the Earth began to slide over it, a hollow of darkness, and they held each other as time seemed to reverse itself. The night sank back into itself, grew darker, deeper. Sunk in timelessness, it seemed they would never have to part. The stars burned more intensely. The shadow of the Earth glowed in its corona.

Then the moon began to swell back into sight. The stars faded. The night lightened, and the sun seemed truly to be pushing them from the other side of the earth. Day was coming. Their last day of summer. The time was coming when they would part.

They might have lain there together in one another's arms until dawn charged pink into the sky, might have made love a third time and a fourth, had the seas not changed underneath them. But the *After You* began to roll in the water, and Riley roused himself to survey the scene. "Must be a storm coming," he told her.

"Should we head in?" It made Clare anxious. She was from a landlocked state, had only read in novels about the perils of stormy seas. She did not want to know firsthand.

"The sky is clear," he said, grazing the horizon all around. "It's probably pushing in from far off. Won't matter."

She had trusted him, and they had stayed until the seas began to buck the boat hard, and it was only then that they noticed the gauze creeping across the full moon, the high haze of clouds advancing before a storm they should have known about, but did not.

The *After You* had plowed hard against the waves, headed toward harbor. Each lurch it took, Clare's stomach felt. Her fingers ached from trying to hold on, trying to keep herself upright.

"No problem," Riley had assured her. "We'll get her home and tucked in. We'll be drinking cocoa in the hotel before anything hits." He laughed. Rough seas were nothing to him. And he had seen so much worse than this, as had his father, his grandfather.

So she had taken his words to heart, been encouraged. After all, by then the *After You* was within sight of Ledgemere. Clare could see the lights of the village scattered around the landing, and rising above it all was the high beam of the lighthouse urging them home.

But they had not made it home. Riley had forgotten about the tides. Not that he didn't know it was low tide. He did. But, in the thrall of their night together, he had failed to work the calculus of moon and wind, stars and tides. He had forgotten to factor in a particular celestial alignment, something rare, which his father and uncles had talked about over Sunday dinner. He wasn't paying the proper kind of attention. He was caught up with how capable he felt, steering his own vessel, bringing Clare safely home. He had forgotten everything but Clare, and he had run his boat aground.

There was a tearing jolt: metal folding back before unflinching rock, the rush of water. "Oh my god," he said, as the boat tilted over onto its side and Clare lost her footing and slid down and away from him. "It must be the eastern ledge," he shouted, reaching for her. It was an underwater ledge, far out in the island harbor. He had gone around it a thousand times in his father's boat at low tide. During high tide, it was no problem. Lobster boats could skim right over it. Now, not only was it low tide, it was a record low tide. If the light had been right, he would have been able to see that the rockweed attached to the ledge was actually showing on the surface.

The wind lashed in their faces, and even though Riley grabbed her to him so quickly that she couldn't see the fear in his eyes, she could feel his heart pounding under his cotton shirt. She could feel his fear all through her.

He cursed the low tide, but he must have known even in those first stark minutes that the high tide would be worse. He must have known that if the rising waves pushed against the boat and if the ledge turned it loose now, the *After You* would sink. And Clare and Riley would be human flotsam on a raging sea. He had not spoken that fear to her, but it must have passed from his pounding heart, circulated into her bloodstream. Because somehow she knew what to fear. She knew.

❧

All these years later, on the stony shore of Ledgemere, she turned her face into his shoulder. Riley wrapped his arms around her, pulled her in close to him, fitting her against the line of him. She tucked her head into the hollow of his neck. She let him hold her.

When she opened her eyes, she saw the stars reflected in the waves, looking as though they were being washed ashore. "Do you ever blame them?" she asked Riley.

"Blame who?"

"The stars . . . for what happened to us out there."

"No," he said. "I blame myself . . . for not reading them right. For not paying attention to the moon hanging out all over the place up there, like a great big traffic signal. Everybody out there knows—or better know—that when the moon is full, the tide is going to go lower and higher than other times. And the way the heavens were scattered out that night, it was even worse."

"And the hurricane," she said, turning where she could see the blue glow of his skin in the starlight. "Don't forget."

"Oh, yeah, the hell ripper," he said.

He lapsed into quiet, and she thought he must remember, as she did, the way the wind had seemed to taunt them as it came up, blowing harder, making it difficult for one to speak to the other. Even Clare knew that no one would hear Riley's sounding of the alarm. No one would hear her cries for help.

The boat was hard aground at first, and then it began to tilt with the rising tide. The wind began to make it buck and shudder. It lurched violently, hit by a wave, and that was the last thing Clare remembered: Riley sliding away from her. Holding on.

Then everything had gone black. When she opened her eyes next, it was to the fluorescent starkness of a hospital room. She did not remember the island men coming out from the harbor in their boats. She did not know that when they were lashing the boats tight in anticipation of the storm, they had noticed the *After You* was missing, nor did she know that they had spotted it in the first gloom of that stormy morning. They had seen it roll in the high tide. They had got hold of Clare. They had found Riley in time.

The ferry had apparently made a dangerous crossing in the rough seas that morning, and from the wharf in Sky Hill, the two teenagers had been airlifted to the hospital. The next day, Riley had been flown all the way to Portland. They had never seen each other again.

Clare had spent two weeks in the hospital. She had broken three ribs and breathed in some water. She suffered from exposure as well as a concussion. That was all. The Prentisses had paid the whole bill, out of affection, maybe, but also out of the conviction that they should have known to govern her better while she was living at Last Look. Riley Brackett was a dear boy to them. They loved his parents. But he had a reckless streak. They should have known. It was like a chorus. Aunt Fran said it. Tig did too. Clare herself thought it. She thought it often. *Should have known.*

It didn't matter. What mattered was that Clare was finally going home—and in time to make amends. Fran and Tig had chastised her for causing pain to her parents at the worst of times, and Clare too blamed herself for this, blamed her love for Riley. When she had first spoken to her mother by phone after the accident, Mom had sobbed, couldn't speak. And Clare could never forget the sight of her father's face when he met her at the airport. He saw the bandages, and his face had crumpled like Kleenex. He had cried.

But she had made it home in time to have some days with her mother. In fact, she had spent them lying on the bed next to her mother, propped on the same pillows, stretched out, holding her hand and sometimes singing "Surrey with the Fringe on Top" or "Supercalifragilistic" or whatever other whimsical tune Mom begged of her. Clare was lying there, holding her hand, when her mother took one torn breath and then no more.

It was natural, after everything that had happened, for Clare to want a reason for her mother's suffering, for her own. She thought of how Mr. Prentiss had bemoaned the astral alignment for creating the tidal trap that Riley had drawn them both into. She thought of Riley himself cursing the moon as they clung to the wrecked hulk of the *After You*. "Damned full moon," he had cried at the capacity of his lungs. "Damned full moon."

So in the long and silent days after her mother slipped away, Clare thought that her mother's death must also have a celestial reason. She began to believe that maybe the night sky somehow held sway over her, that if she could only read the heavens, she could know what to be wary of. She could know which direction to go, which to avoid.

Not even a week after her mother's funeral, Clare had asked her father for a book on astronomy. Late at night, when she couldn't sleep, she turned on the light and read from its pages. She read about a cluster of stars called Praesepe, which looked like a fuzzy cloud to her, but to the ancients it had seemed like a thin spot in the floor of heaven. They called it the "gates of men" because it was where souls descended to Earth to be born. Did souls ascend through it too? she wondered. Had her mother gone that way?

Such thoughts only tormented her, and she tried to blot them with the science. She memorized the order of the universe: the sun orbiting the Milky Way nucleus, the Earth and other planets orbiting the sun, and the solar system completing one orbit of the galaxy every two-hundred-and-twenty million years. There was comfort in these vast, mind-evading numbers. There was comfort in distance measured by traveling light, in temperature measured by color. The hottest stars, she had learned, were not red but blue.

The worst nights, when nothing in the cosmological facts eased her, she went out into the pasture behind the house and lay in the rough grass. And lying there with her face to the sky, she thought of Riley. She understood that sometimes the stars she could see from Earth were nothing but light from stars that had already gone out, nothing but a ghost of what had once blazed. That was the way she tried to imagine him, far away and already extinguished. Their love had blazed out.

But why then could she still see the red of his hair, feel the fine sandpaper of his fingertips on her most tender skin, taste his seawater kiss? Why was he always there, why was she in his arms, why were the two of them just as they had been? Why were they still—every passing night, every moving hour—why were they still like a star burning blue?

ᴖᴗ

Riley shifted on their rock, gathered Clare closer to him. Seventeen years had interleaved their last moments together and this, but those years might not have existed now. He was as real to her as he had once been.

She must have always remained this real to him, she thought. At first, he must still have believed that their love for each other would bring her back. No matter how things had ended that summer, she would come back. It was not such a ludicrous thing to believe, if he allowed himself to remember what they had shared.

She just never had allowed herself that. It had been easier to try and forget him. To spare herself. To spare her family. So she had never answered any of his letters. She had not come to the phone the one time he called long distance.

Eventually, she had worked her way to a fresh beginning. But he had had no choice but to go on living in the shadow of where she had been, where everything was the same except for her absence; the tides still rose and fell by the pull of the moon, the trees still turned red and yellow in Sky Hill, the birds going south still stopped over on Ledgemere. Her absence must have loomed over everything he did. To him, she became what might have been. She became what should have been.

One night, one lunar eclipse had pointed them in different directions. It might have happened that way in any case—they might have parted. Surely they would have. But it might have happened in a way that made it possible for each of them to make progress. One might not have had to run. The other might not have had to cling to one happy promise. They might each have carried the memory of one another, not as a burden but as a blessing, a lesson in love, a place to begin: he in his way, she in hers.

And who or what was to blame that they hadn't? Was it the full moon? Or was it the threat of her mother's death that had driven them so deeply, desperately into one another? Was it nothing but young lust? What was to blame for that moment that tore them apart and yet left them forever bound to each other?

Clare shuddered. "You can never know, can you?" she whispered, feeling herself to be the girl she had been then, feeling the fear that did not belong to one moment or another but to all the unguarded hours when she suddenly understood what the real possibilities were. It might happen when she clipped a rose from the bush and found the mildew beginning on a leaf, or when she saw a falling star flare and disappear forever. When she noticed a certain shadow under her eyes and knew, remembered, dreaded.

One moment could change everything.

Everything was random. Everything she knew, everything any-one knew, was nothing more than cosmic debris, scattered in the universe by one explosion of hydrogen, and all of it was connected only by light, nothing but tenuous light. The sun slowly burning out, the moon with its dark side, the stars blinking from light-years away, the Earth revolving blue in its orbit, and its mountains in Africa, in Asia, in all the Americas, its forests and its islands, its oceans hearkening to lunar attraction, its sunsets, its sunrises, its eclipses. It was all such a deceptive order. It was all born of chaos and was subject to it always, as were each of the planets in their prescribed orbits around our solitary star, as were the quasars pulsing at the edge of distant black holes, as were the seasons burgeoning and dying back to burgeon again, as were our very cells circulating in warm blood, our very organs twitching to our breathing, our cleansing, our loving, and also our dearest hopes, desires, beliefs sizzling from synapse to synapse. All merely cosmic debris.

"What's that?" Riley's lips moved against her forehead.

Clare could never hope to make him understand. She could never make anyone understand. She herself could not understand wholly. All she said, all she could say, was, "You can never know what's going to change you forever. What's going to happen that will never let you go."

He paused for a long moment. He exhaled a long breath and broke it off with one flint syllable: "No."

Hours passed, and the night sky shifted. The ocean retreated toward low tide. They didn't speak, only leaned into one another, shoulder-to-shoulder, holding one another up as each fought the insupportable thoughts.

Later, Clare was startled to hear his voice, as she was startled to see the moon gone from the east to farther west. How long would it have taken for the Earth to have tilted this far? "You're shivering," was what he said. "Let's get you home."

He kept his arm around her as they walked toward the mound of the high land, leaving the gray ocean and coming into the black shade of the trees, into the aroma of the balsams. She stopped and breathed deeply.

Riley was invisible to her. At that moment, he was only the woolen fabric of his sleeve, where her fingers clung to the bend in his elbow. He was only a hovering warmth in the cool night. She could not see him when his lips closed on hers, could not see him as he kissed her as though he were drinking a long draft. He was a shadow in the dark.

She pulled away, closed her eyes.

"I'm sorry," he said.

She found him again. He was not an inch away, his lips, his mouth. She kissed him, and his arms tightened around her, pulled her onto the tips of her toes, off the ground entirely so that she dangled in his embrace as though through some magnetism that had nothing to do with the muscles of his arms, nothing to do with his strong back or his solid legs. He held her.

Their breathing seemed shared. She breathed him. She felt him take her breath inside himself. She was becoming only his exhalations, only the sigh of him.

He pulled away, laid his temple against hers. His heart beat there, hard and racing. Held in his arms, pressed to him, her whole being rose and fell as his chest rose and fell. She floated on him. "Clare," he said. "Clare Mac."

Her teeth began to chatter. She did not feel cold. She was flushed through with heat. He put her soles back down on the needles of the path. The ground did not feel solid to her. She seemed to sink.

He took her hand, though, led her along the dark path. It widened, became the road into town. Out of the darkness, she could see the faint white of painted shutters and doors. Certain flowers seemed to glow in the starlight. Otherwise, it was dark. Kerosene lights had been extinguished, candles blown out. Where their two hands met—Clare's and Riley's—that union seemed a point of light. It seemed the only lit thing in the village.

Passing the door to the hotel, he led her along the porch and then down the side steps onto the lawn. He cut an angle across it.

The high beam of the lighthouse winked toward the sea, swept like sight over their heads. They turned the corner. She saw his other hand rise toward the doorknob of his cottage.

As soon as they were inside, he dipped his head to her neck and moved his lips up behind her ear, over it, across her temple, her forehead, down her nose to her upper lip, to her mouth. She arched into him, yearning, and he lifted her like a child and carried her up the stairs.

It was a narrow mattress, and he settled her against the wall, lay down next to her, along the length of her, close. Her legs laced through his, and her fingers were in the rough coils of hair behind his ears. She touched lightly the ridge of his cheekbone, the closed convexity of his eyelids, the brush of his eyelashes. His skin grew damp. He breathed steam across her earlobe, and it rushed like the sound of the ocean deep inside her. She moaned in answer to it, echoing. He breathed across the hollow of her neck, out into the cup of her breastbone, which seemed to hold his breath like water, to save it until it pooled and chilled and made her shiver with what she wanted.

He laid the palm of his hand against her neck, and she felt the flat heat coming from the swirls of his lined palm, the perfect constellations of his fingerprints. He touched her where the stem of her neck met her shoulder. The fingers slid down into the split of her shirt, moving at the buttons: Riley's fingers, the stars at his fingertips, the celestial map of his hand.

Lifting her hand to his, Clare pressed her palm flush against his, laid each of her fingers to his, the lines of one crosshatching the other: stopping him.

She began to cry. She had followed his fingers in their pursuit, had read their intent and urged them on. She had wanted nothing more than his touch. Nothing more than for him to lay himself over her, to rise between her and the night sky.

But now she reached to halt him, to twine her own fingers

through his and stop him, just stop him. Suddenly she knew: All the years had coming crashing down, collapsing like paper houses into this moment, into this hour in her life. She was thirty-four years old, and she had survived cancer so far, and his fingertips would find only scar tissue, only what was left. She was not who she had been.

Not even Riley, who had touched her there first, not even he could touch her and make her whole. Once, he had given her the power of her own skin, her lips, her breasts. That power was gone. He could not give it back to her. No one could give it to her.

"Clare," he breathed, still not knowing, thinking she was stirred to tears by her passion, by her love. His voice seemed to come from far down in him.

She turned toward the wall, doubled into her grief. She sobbed. She could not go back for what she wanted. Reality barred her way. She could only go forward. She had to find the way forward.

"Clare?" he asked tenderly, concern soft over the thick huskiness in his voice that still bore the burden of his desire. His big hand cupped her shoulder. It moved down her arm, squeezed as he grew more aware of her pain. He sat up next to her, pulled her onto his lap, keened exhalations into her hair.

"Clare," he said, not even asking anymore, only comforting. "Clare, Clare, Clare," like a lullaby, like playing waves on his guitar: washing, coming again, washing, washing away. Because Riley knew too, knew in the only way he could. She thought he must. He must know now, as she had learned, that there were things you couldn't say, feelings that didn't have words made for them yet, kinds of pain, forms of longing, variations of love. He held her as she cried, and she cried harder still because she had no words to tell him why. She could not find the shape of them, could not think how they might start or what sound they might make escaping into the black still air of this room, into the warm-breathed space between them. She could not think what punctuation would measure them. She had no words.

The next morning, Clare waved good-bye to Riley from the ferry.
He wouldn't really look at her, and only cut his arm through the
air once, a sort of abbreviated gesture. He looked forlorn. His
feelings were in the very cast of his shoulders, which she could see
long after she lost the expression of his face. She could see it as
long as she could see the crazy blaze of his hair. He did not turn
and head back up the hill into the village. He stood rooted.

Earlier she had crawled from the crevice where she had slept,
between the slab of the wall and Riley's warm bulk. His breath
was coming evenly, each exhalation evaporating in a little whistle.
His face was slack as a child's, exhausted, and she fought the
impulse to lay her fingers against his temple. Instead she had

stepped into her shoes, pulling on her sweater as she tiptoed down the stairs. She managed to pull the door quietly closed behind her.

The sky had only begun to blush in the east, and the outside air was cold as well water. Dew was threaded like beads on each stalk of grass. Clare bent her head into her escape, went around the corner of the cottage, and nearly collided with Laurie Brackett's sister.

Clare jolted upright, startled to the quick.

Kim was holding a plate of muffins. They were still hot enough to steam. Clare could smell the burred sweetness of nutmeg. Bringing him muffins was exactly the kind of gesture on his sister-in-law's part that drove Riley nuts. "She's just reporting back to the home office," he had groused to Clare only yesterday.

Clare's hand went self-consciously to her hair. It looked as though she had spent a night tossing on passion. "Kim," she said. "G'morning."

"Good morning," Kim answered. Her expression was taut with judgment.

"We were talking late," Clare said, ashamed even to have to make an excuse.

A rustling came from Riley's room. He hung out the window. "Hey, Kimmie," he said. "You're up early."

"Yeah," his sister-in-law answered. "And you look like you've been up all night."

Clare had started across the lawn then, acting as though she were a minor player in a scene, acting as if she could slip unnoticed offstage. "Where're you going, Clare?" Riley called after her, ignoring his sister-in-law.

"Home," she said. "I have to catch the first ferry."

He had spent the rest of the morning trying to get her alone and, failing that, trying to extract some promise from her. When they were standing at the landing, and the ferry was churning its way toward them, he had asked if she loved him. Though he whispered, his voice was iron in his conviction that she did. It was a challenge. "Don't you?"

He had caught her arm as she turned to look back across the rolling wake of the boat, down the path toward the mainland, toward her life. She had avoided his eyes, but he had outlasted her. She told him finally, chose her words carefully, measured out their consequences: "There is a certain love I have for you, yes, Riley," she told him softly. "In that way, I love you very much. Yes."

"Don't talk down to me," he told her. He didn't say it harshly. "I'm not a kid. I just happen to have the memory of one." He said it with resignation.

They stood there longer. The sun was going in and out of clouds. For the time it took one cloud to pass, they said nothing. Behind them, the ferry docked.

"Do you have to go this way?" he asked. "Just bolt?"

"I have to," she said.

"Why do you have to?"

"After last night . . ." she tried.

"Nothing happened last night," he said. "We didn't . . ."

"Is that what you think?" she asked. "Do you think nothing happened last night?"

He looked at her deeply, then shook his head. She turned to watch Captain Barnicle tie up.

Riley asked, "Are you coming back?"

"Someday," she said.

"Don't do me any favors," he said, and when she had flinched from his pain, from her role in it, he softened. He pulled her then against him—in front of the crowd gathered to greet someone from the ferry or to board it themselves, in front of the crowd drawn by the rumor that Riley was here with Clare, out in the open. He held her and rubbed his chin against her hair so that she felt his morning stubble on her scalp. It made her shiver. He kissed her good-bye there where his chin had rubbed, as though he had softened up a place on her, a place through which she might absorb his best intentions and all his true feeling.

—◌◌—

Captain Barnicle came and stood next to her at the rail, after they were halfway back to Sky Hill. "You look as bad as he did," he said, by way of questioning her without questioning her.

She shrugged, wondering if Kim's discovery had spread to him yet. Probably not. He wouldn't be so friendly if he had heard. "Seeing me didn't do him any good," she said.

"Didn't do you any favors that I can see," he observed.

"It's sad," she said. Then she guiltily searched for some way to make her feelings something universal and not something particular, to make it not what it was: regret at leaving Riley, shame for needing to leave him. "Everybody suspects he's playing at it," she told the captain. "But he's not. He'd be the happiest guy around if it would all just click back into place."

"Anybody who saw him the day he had the accident can put the oakum to that nonsense. Doc worked on him from the time they got him over to the Ledgemere landing and all the way over on the ferry. We couldn't rouse a coast guard chopper, and I had to run Riley all the way in. I thought it was going to be me who had to go tell Laurie that he was gone. But he hung on."

"Laurie said he got tangled in his winch."

The captain nodded. "Happens to the best of them. They're out there alone, get a little lax, and get twisted up in their line. And over they go. We had a guy here last year who cut his arm off to get loose. He's out there now, still lobstering." He whistled in admiration, then said, "Riley was lucky Carn Libby was hauling within sight of him because, going over, his head smashed open. Knocked him cold. He would have drowned for sure. But Carn got there."

"God, he's star-crossed and blessed at the same time."

Captain Barnicle agreed. "Some folks have got that luck. Others have got none at all." He paused, looked out over the wake for a long minute, then said, "Well, it was good of you to try and help him. That's what matters." He smiled at her, and she smiled back. And after they had pulled into the harbor at Sky Hill and had tied up at the landing, Captain Barnicle took Clare's bag and walked her to the Saturn.

"Come back sometime," he said as she seated herself behind the wheel. "It's bound to get better. And you don't want to have to remember him this way."

It was what her father had told her that morning he had driven her to the airport for her flight to Maine. She had pleaded one last time to stay home, and he had sighed and let it be known that he had exhausted his tolerance. "You don't want to remember her that way," he had said flatly, all his kindness ground down, blown away. She had felt slapped. Who was he to tell her what memories she should and shouldn't have?

It was only years later that she wondered if he hadn't been right. There were things that existed in her mind, images that presented themselves whole sometimes, horribly whole. A sound could trigger them, or a smell. Once, when Michael had split open a watermelon and held out a chunk for her, she had caught the fresh pink scent of it, and in an instant had seen her mother lying in bed with her skin draped around her wrists and loose on her fingers. Clare had fed her pieces of watermelon, bite by bite, those final days. "More salt," her mother would say. "More salt." And Clare would shake more onto each piece and hold it to her mother's broken lips, and her mother would suck on it as though it were a piece of ice, as though she were waiting for it to melt and spare her the pain of swallowing it.

Clare could have lived forever without seeing her mother waste away like that. Her father had been right. And now she would live forever seeing it. It was always there. She thought about those shadows always twitching at the back of her consciousness when she was roughest with Michael. Sometimes she just wanted to throw herself down in front of him, a flesh-and-blood barrier between him and the worst of human suffering. Sometimes she just wanted to keep him from all that. Del had accused her of selfishness for such behavior. She had accused Clare of not caring.

If anything, she cared too much.

Protection. It came down to protection. Ever since her mother had died, she had been desperate to protect—herself, those she loved. But she couldn't do it. No one could.

But there was the approximation of Riley. With him came some old association of rescue. Certainly it had been an illusion even then. He had assuaged her fears, distracted her from terror all summer, and then, unwittingly, he had come close to killing her. Despite that, or maybe because of it—because they had faced the maw together and survived—he still meant protection.

She had needed to leave him today. Because she had wanted to stay.

This morning when she woke, she had wanted to roll over, curl into him, and let him curve his body around hers, hold her. She had wanted to say, "I had cancer, and I can't stop being afraid. I'm always so scared."

But she could not say it. She could not say it. There was the question of Michael.

Her thoughts braked on that: the question of Michael. How had those two words come to be linked—question and Michael? He had been for years the one certainty in her life. Her career was a frenetic obstacle course. Her relationship with her father was wracked with guilt, both his and hers. Her health had been precarious. But there had always been Michael. There had always been Michael to make her oatmeal in the middle of the night when she couldn't sleep, oatmeal swirled with a spoonful of raspberry jam. There had always been Michael to touch in the dusk of early morning when she woke to her fears, Michael to reach for, Michael to hold. There always had been. Before.

⌒⌒⌒

On impulse, almost as a way to stop the whir of her thoughts, she pulled in at the Churchhouse farmstand and bought quarts of strawberries. The farmer threw in a dozen extra. "They'll go to waste," the woman had said, carrying them to the car herself. Driving, Clare could smell them in the backseat, fresh and simple.

At sunset, she crossed the long bridge over into New Hampshire. The sky was rose-gold beyond the green steel arches overhead, and she thought how she had seen the other pink this morning, the day beginning. It had seemed longer than one day, longer even than a summer day in Maine: coming away.

And she still had a stretch of night before her, a long distance to go. She figured eight hours at least for the entire trip. The logical thing would be to pull into River Port for the night, break it up, drive tomorrow when she was rested. But she couldn't face Michael. Not yet. She couldn't face the tension that would harden his jaw, nor could she face how he would try to work it free, would fight against it. She couldn't face what he would do to her in that moment. She couldn't face what she had done to him.

She needed her flowers, her garden. She needed to dig in the soil, wallow a little in how close she had come to betraying him— or was it more than close? She needed to know what she felt— about Michael, about Riley, about herself. Before she saw Michael, she had to work back to herself, back into her own skin, her own existence.

It was midnight when she pulled into the driveway at home. She stood in the grass of the yard in her bare feet and went to look at her flowers in the streetlight. It was as though she were looking at them through pond water, through a sheen of pale green. The scent of the roses was sharp as spice in the night air, and the insects whirred on and on, as though she were not even there.

She unlocked the door. The house smelled of Murphy's Oil Soap and flowers gone stale in their vases. She opened all the windows, turned on the ceiling fan, and went to the machine. It blinked with six messages. They were all from Riley. The gist of each was, "Come back. Please, come back."

She erased them one by one.

The next morning, she woke early. She had been dreaming about Riley. He was standing on the rocks, reciting something from Shakespeare, a passage that she could not bring into the light of day. She rolled over heavily in the bed and laid her hand on Michael's pillow. She spread her fingers where his head should have been.

"Three days," she told herself. She had to get through three days, and then Michael would be home to accompany her to the checkup. It was a bad reason to have him back. But it was reason enough. She would put the madness behind her. She would leave Riley where he belonged.

Clare stemmed the berries on the front porch while the daytime bugs sawed all around the house, the sizzle of somnolent heat. At dusk, she went to stand over the stove. The aroma rose up out of the enamel pot like sweet smoke, and Clare was still there late into the night, tired, as she boiled the berries down in batches, thickened them, ladled them into hot jars, and let them steam in a hot bath.

Riley called three times, the last time after she had showered and slipped into bed. She had thought she would sleep easily. She had thought she had spent herself on her tasks, boiled herself down to exhaustion and certain rest. But her mind was restless. It wandered. She found herself in Maine, looking at the stars, leaning into him. She found herself kissing him.

When the phone rang, she held the cordless in the palm of her hand, let it vibrate. Her room was dark except for the haze of the streetlight down the block, and the sudden light of the phone pulsing red, like urgency. She let the machine pick up, though her thumb hovered over the answer button, wanting to complete the connection, wanting to lie in the darkness and tell him what she had held back, tell him what she had carried away with her, packing it off the island as she had packed it on: her burden.

She could imagine him now on the porch of the general store standing in the island darkness, the glow of his skin seeming to give off light with its paleness. Maybe he was standing by the liars' bench, where she had stood two nights before making her own call. He would be hearing the huffing ocean as it lapped around the pilings. He would hear the music. Someone somewhere would surely be singing.

Why couldn't it be Michael calling? She tried to imagine Michael's face, tried to recall the scent of his skin. But she couldn't. She'd been kept out so long. She couldn't make it come out right. She couldn't hear the timbre of his voice, the rhythm of his inflections.

Anyway, it was Riley's voice that came out of the machine, a genie out of its box. "Good night, Clare Mac." He hesitated, and she hung on for the rest, prayed it into being. "That's all. I just wanted you to know . . . good night."

The machine clicked and rewound and clicked. *Michael,* she chanted to herself. She closed her eyes. *Three more days to Michael.* She tried again to sleep.

Three nights later, Michael called. It was six o'clock, and Clare was expecting him to pull in the driveway at any minute. She had showered and put on a sleeveless summer dress that he loved to see her wear. The water was boiling for pasta, the garlic was minced, the shrimp peeled.

She answered the phone with foreboding. Really, she had been expecting this call all afternoon. His mother's day had been a hard one, he explained, and he hadn't gotten on the road when he had wanted. Exhaustion weighed in his voice.

"Stay," she told him. "Meet me there in the morning, at ten. It'll be easier on you."

"And you?" he said.

"Don't worry about me." She hated herself for saying it. She knew it was disingenuous. Even her blood screamed, *Worry about me. Hold my hand*. But something else in her wanted him to figure things out on his own. If she had to prompt him to give her what she needed, it wasn't worth having. That had been the beauty of their relationship always, the naturally synchronized give-and-take, the dance. It was all she wanted from him—what she had always had.

———᥍———

The next morning, she swung the Saturn into the hospital's parking lot five minutes early and scanned every space looking for the Explorer. It wasn't here. He wasn't here yet. She'd wait out here in the car, she thought, get a quick peck on the cheek at least, walk in under his power as much as her own. She watched a blue jay tussle with a piece of American-cheese sandwich that someone had dropped on the pavement.

It was five minutes past the hour of her appointment when she finally locked the car and went into the office. The receptionist, a prematurely gray-haired woman named Lily, greeted her warmly. Her eyes touched the air over Clare's shoulder, but she didn't ask about Michael. They learned tactfulness in this job, Clare suspected. People vanished, in one way or another.

Clare undressed, and a phlebotomist took blood. And before she had time to grow impatient, Dr. Bladoe was there with his kindly, soft hands, the fingers with the dark hair that stood up between the knuckles, the smell of peppermint. He touched her hand in greeting, and before he began the examination, he asked his questions, looking her in the eyes with each one. Then, laying her back on the loud paper, his hands moved over her body slowly, finding the outlines of her organs, rolling around them, thumping them like drums. The thought ran through her: *what he sees with-out his eyes . . . what he sees without his eyes . . .* She wasn't going anywhere with the thought. She was just letting it loop, taking the distraction of banality.

When he had her sitting up and breathing for his stethoscope, he finally patted her on the shoulder and spoke hope in simple ways, and she felt like a child. She found she did not resent the feeling. He was a caring man. He had taken care of her on morn-ings when she had wanted to keep her eyes closed, when she had not wanted to see what waited. He would take care of her again if it came to that. It struck her, vaguely and without impact, that her feeling toward him in this moment, so submissive, was an abyss removed from that of the defiant young woman she had been a year ago, challenging him with studies on shark cartilage and low serum retinol and lactobacillus acidophilus. She had crossed over the abyss since then. She had looked down.

The doctor walked her to the big cool rooms where the equip-ment hummed, and where she always thought of NASA and the dark weightless reaches of space, where she always imagined that the blue earth was suspended far away. She lay still in the clasp of each machine, heard it whir and click, gossiping to itself over the secrets of her muscles, her bones, the course of her blood. She tried to float above herself, like the Earth in space, tried to re-member the way the stars were arranged in the August sky if you looked west or north, if you looked south or east. She tried to suspend herself in darkness and stardust.

⟿

At the end of the afternoon, as Dr. Bladoe led her back into his office, she glimpsed Michael down a long hallway. His back was turned, and she didn't acknowledge that she had seen him because, even as she felt herself stir toward him, she felt the recoil too, the flinching away. When the door was closed between her and her husband, she broke down suddenly.

She was sitting across from her doctor. In all the time of her illness and its aftermath, she could not recall letting her tears loose in front of Dr. Bladoe. Not on the day he told her the biopsy results. Not on the day of the surgery. Not on the day when she had to go back and try to forget enough to live.

"It's unlikely we'll find anything, Clare," he reassured her now, politely glancing away from her tears. "You look to be in the pink physically. You've had no pain, no signs at all."

"Okay," she said, blowing her nose and wiping desperately at the tears. "I know. I feel great."

"That's very convincing," he said in a tone of mild sarcasm that made her smile and then dissolve again. Her shoulders moved in involuntary spasms. She sobbed.

Lily tapped on the door and peeked in. "Michael's in the waiting room," she told Clare.

Clare wadded the Kleenex in her hand, dabbed it at her nose hard, and said, "Could you please tell him everything's gone well, and ask him just to meet me at home?"

The woman hesitated.

Clare added, "I know he's had a long day."

Lily nodded and disappeared behind the snap of the closing door, and Dr. Bladoe manufactured a light tone, as if the modulation of his vocal cords could restore an emotional balance to the room. "Still reading those books of yours?" he asked.

Clare managed a bleak smile, shook her head. She could not look at him. "I gave them up," she said. "Because one night I was reading along, and it said that cancer was the disease of timing."

"Timing?"

She nodded. "It waits for a time when you're dealing with the past, with everything that's hurt you. And then it takes you. That's what the book said."

The doctor whistled through his front teeth. She thought it was because he didn't know in the slightest how to respond to that statement, to her pain, to a sense of disease so far beyond the lab where he had worked over the cadaver of a sixty-seven-year-old stranger, so far beyond the gray-tile corridors of the hospital where he had done his numbing rotations, so far beyond the scalpel and the cauterizing lasers and his own worn copy of the *Merck Manual*.

Clare couldn't stop: "And I guess I couldn't stand that thought. It's one thing to think that I got it because my mom had it, and it's programmed into my genes: immutable. It's one thing to think that it was because I didn't have a baby at a young enough age, so true to the survival of the fittest, the old useless one with no function in the continuum of the species gets shunted: pure niggardly science. It's one thing to blame myself for mountain-biking under electric wires or eating too many red M&M's or drinking two glasses of wine instead of one. That seems arbitrary and simple somehow: stupid cause and effect. But to think that it came from the things that hurt me most, the things I can't let go of, that was more than I could take. I couldn't stand to think that it had preyed on my vulnerabilities, mine, the same ones that make me cry in the middle of the night. I couldn't stand to think that it was that personal. Do you know?"

The doctor was of a different generation, her father's. He could count her white blood cells and monitor the pressure of her blood flow and touch her most intimate skin with dispassion. He could use his kind tone. He could pat her hand in authoritative comfort. But he was only a doctor. He could not touch her pain. He cleared his throat, seemed to reach, to ask anything that would change the subject: "Have you given any more consideration to the reconstructive surgery?"

She struggled. "It cut something out of me that I can't recon-struct," she said. "Something here." She touched her heart. "I've lost. . . . I can't find anyone who can give me back what I've lost. Having breasts again won't make me whole."

The doctor cleared his throat. "You're going to be just fine, Clare," he said, standing up and laying a hand on her shoulder again. By rote, she thought. His kindness was practiced. She was grateful for it, had always been grateful for it. He had made the effort to learn it when other health-care professionals hadn't both-ered. But at the same, he had learned it, had been taught. He had practiced perfecting it as surely as he had practiced the techniques of medicine. And sometimes, like medicine, it wasn't enough. "You're going to be in the pink," he said again.

"Okay," she answered. But she couldn't stop crying.

ᐸᑐ

At home, Michael was making cookies: a peace offering. She could smell them when she opened the back gate. He swung the screen door open and came down the flagstones and reached for her. She laid her face flat against the fine weave of his shirt. She closed her sore eyes, inhaled him.

"I'm so sorry," he said.

She kissed him on the underside of his jaw. "Don't be," she said. Her voice was still bruised-sounding from the crying, and she hoped he wouldn't notice. She felt ashamed by her meltdown.

"Did it go all right?" She could hear the fear in him, though he tried to toss it off with nonchalance, as though it were a fore-gone conclusion: She was healthy.

"I got through it. We'll know sometime next week if I'm clean."

"You are," he said, not allowing any other possibility, tightening his embrace.

She sighed. "That would be convenient, wouldn't it?"

He held her away from him, looked at her. "What's that supposed to mean, Clare?"

She shook her head, shoved back from her implication, shoved back from starting anything. After all, he was home. "It's been a long day," she said. "Don't pay any attention to me."

"Sweet girl," he said and kissed her forehead. His lips against her skin moved, saying, "I baked you cookies. JoJo's recipe, the one with three cups of chocolate chips."

"Did you bake it all?"

They sat in the porch swing. She ate a spoonful of raw dough, and he ate warm cookies dunked in a mug of milk. Chocolate dripped down his chin, and she tried to nibble at it, which tickled him so that he giggled and seemed himself at last, for the first time in the longest time. She swung her legs up over his and cuddled him. "I missed you so much," she said, nipping at his collarbone.

"I missed you," he said, but his voice seemed to fade as he said it, as his mind wandered back to why he had been away, to that unswayable fact of his life: his mother's illness.

They swung back and forth in the swing, and the sun began to go down over the river, and soon the current ran orange. Clare thought how pain was like a room. Hers had doors and windows. Riley's did too. But Michael was closed up in his, locked away.

"Is it bad?" she asked, trying any way to get inside with him.

He shuddered, as if reentering with difficulty the dimension of time and space where she was. "What?" he asked.

"Mommy Belle?"

"Bad, yes," he said. "It's bad."

Clare wanted to ask what stage of bad. She wanted to know about the time left. About what was next. But she couldn't ask him that. She reminded herself why she couldn't. To her, his mother's illness had become a kind of prison, a place where they all suffered. And she was always wanting to know: How much longer? How long until the agony ended?

But that was saying, *How much longer will your mother live?* The thought clanged in her like a terrible bell. She burned with the shame of it. When will your mother die? When can I have you back? When can you return to yourself? She was horrible even to herself.

How had it come to this? she wondered. How had this disease so divided them that she could no longer use his pain as her guidance in compassion? There was his experience of it. There was hers. There was an unnatural chasm between them—unnatural to two people who loved one another.

"Why don't you cry?" she asked him. The accusation in the question startled even her. She went rigid at his side.

The rigidity seemed to enter him, through her. "What does that mean?"

"Why don't you ever let it out?"

"What?"

She groaned at his elusiveness. "Whatever it is you're feeling about your mother."

"I do," he said defensively.

"Where?" she cried. "In the shower? In the car on I-95? Why don't you ever cry with me?"

"I can't do anything right," he said. He stood up and walked to the railing, held onto it with a white grip. "Everybody needs something from me, and I don't ever seem to get it right."

"I need to help you," she said softly.

He shot her a fierce look, something feral and cornered. "You need to see me suffer?"

She brought her palms down hard on the slats of the swing. "Michael," she said. "If you don't let me know how you're feeling, I can't feel it with you. I can't feel sorry for anyone—except myself, because I'm losing you."

"I don't need your pity."

"I don't want to pity you, Michael. I just want to go through it with you. I want to be with you. I want to feel it with you."

"You can't feel this," he said. "You shouldn't have to."

"I want to," she said, coming to stand next to him. "I need to."

"Just let me be strong," he said, sieving the words through gritted teeth. But there was a fragility to his voice. He could not disguise it from her.

She laid a hand over his. "You don't have to be strong with me," she said. "I need you not to be strong all the time."

"Clare," he said, opening his mouth to go on, then closing it. She saw him surrender to his own needs, saw him reject hers. She saw too how this pivot away from her pained him. Still, in one torn motion, he turned and walked past her, through the screen door into the house, past the piano room, past the kitchen, and into the bedroom. He closed the door behind him.

Part Three

Sitting on a bench in Central Park, Clare told JoJo: "So there was silence all night and silence all the next day, and then Del called, and I knew Michael was going to leave. So I left. To go back to Maine. To see Riley. And that's when, by some fluke, I picked up the tape."

JoJo jumped as if stung. She yelped. "Damn!"

"What?" Clare asked, alarmed.

"Damned cell phone's going off," JoJo said. "It's like carrying your vibrator around in your purse.... Hello?"

Clare watched the pigeons as JoJo talked to her office. As roommates, the two of them had frequented this same bench years before. It was toward the south end of the park, and from it you could hear the traffic roaring around Columbus Circle like rapids around a boulder. There were gray rocks behind them, and in the distance, over the ruffle of treetops, she could see the apartment houses along Fifth Avenue. The afternoon was slanted across their pink and brown and white granite faces, shadows thrown long from their marble balconies.

JoJo had her legs crossed, and one elegant SoHo pump was dangling off her toe, swinging back and forth. Her DKNY outfit was strewn with crumbs because for the past half-hour they had been eating potato-chip sandwiches. Even as JoJo commanded the phone conversation with professional brio, she was holding her fourth sandwich: two potato chips with a square of Hershey chocolate clamped between them. Comfort food. They had hit on the combination in their bagel days, the time early in their careers when they had eaten thirty-cent bagels for breakfast and for lunch and sometimes for dinner too. Chocolate was their splurge, their salvation. "The salt of the chips amplifies the potency of the Hershey's," JoJo had claimed, and though they had since invoked the mere memory of the combination to amuse and disgust people at fancy cocktail parties, today they had darted into a Korean grocery on Broadway and brought along the makings anyway. "For old times' sake," Jo had said.

Clare pulled her legs up under her now, sat cross-legged on the bench. Potato-chip sandwiches or not, she had longed for the comfort of JoJo's company, but she had forgotten how much it could help: telling all. She turned to face JoJo, who fed her the sandwich, despite the fact that Clare tried to ward it off with both palms.

JoJo hung up. "What tape?" she asked.

Clare was busy with the chips, which were sharp against the roof of her mouth.

"What tape?" JoJo urged.

Clare swallowed. "We were already miles apart, emotionally

anyway, and then the mommies called the next morning," she said, backing up to get a good run at her story.

"You know," JoJo mused. "There are very few unattractive things about The Michael. But I have to say that the "mommies" thing is pretty distracting. I don't know how you ever got past the fact that your guy was calling somebody mommy."

"*Two* somebodies mommy."

"Exactly." Jo kept her eyebrow cocked.

"I forgave him a lot of things. Maybe I thought it was cute." Clare shrugged.

JoJo grimaced.

"This from a woman who is eating her fifth potato-chip-and-Hershey sandwich."

"Ummmm," Jo hummed blissfully, her mouth full. She rolled her hand as she did in the editing room when she wanted the tape to start again.

Clare said, "So Del called with the crisis of the day. I shouldn't be flip about it, I know. But I'm trying to give you the spirit of the thing. Where I was that day."

JoJo nodded.

"I could tell by the way Michael came back into the room that he was going to get in his car and go right back up there. And, call me selfish, but I had two more weeks left away from the network, and I wanted to spend them with him. I wanted to make something of them. Look, I'd been away from home literally from the day I finished the radiation therapy. Five months."

"You wanted it," JoJo said defensively. She had been the one responsible for making sure that Clare got the trial-in-L.A. assignment. Other execs at the network had been worried about whether Clare would be up for it, given the cancer and its treatment. But Clare had begged. "Forget my body, Jo. My head needs this."

"Of course I wanted it," Clare reassured JoJo now. "But by this point, I wanted my life back. I wanted my husband back."

"Of course," JoJo murmured.

"I mean, there's nothing he can do there, Jo, besides everything. All he's doing is just making it possible for Del *not* to do what needs to be done. It's unrealistic that Belle should be at home this late in her illness. It's madness. It's dangerous. They can't control her. They can't get her to eat sometimes. They can't keep her clean. But Del can't bear the thought of anything else. She also can't bear the burden. Not by herself. So Michael ends up trying." She sighed and closed her eyes a minute and remembered how her frustration had come to a crescendo, how it had obliterated every good impulse she had.

"And so when he came in the room that way . . . with *leaving* all over him . . . I lost it. I just said, Look, don't tell me you're leaving, okay? Because *I'm* leaving."

JoJo inhaled sharply.

"And I did. I got in the car with a duffel of clothes and a bag of tapes and some cookies left over from the day before, and that was it."

"You left him?"

Clare nodded solemnly. "I couldn't take it anymore, Jo. I was tired of feeling sorry for myself because I wasn't allowed to feel sorry for him, and I had been trying to stop thinking about Riley but I couldn't stop thinking about Riley. And it was the only thing that made sense: Go to Riley. At least he could admit he was a mess. We could be a mess together. It was a completely irrational thing. But I couldn't just sit there and see how far apart Michael and I had grown. I couldn't take that."

JoJo wasn't eating anymore. She was waiting.

"Only I heard the tape before I got there." She described for JoJo how she had groped around for something to play and had

come across the recording she had made of Garrison Keillor singing "Down in the Valley," the tape on which she had accidentally
recorded her conversation with Michael years before. "And that
made me think about daisy chains."

"Daisy chains?" JoJo asked. "As in that gay thing?"

"No." Clare was suddenly irritated by JoJo's need to leaven
everything with wit. Jo was too embarrassed to show her real
feelings. She never cried. Never. When they had gone to see *A
River Runs Through It,* Clare had wept inconsolably into her
sweater sleeve, while her friend had wisecracked at all the heartbreaking moments. Jo was the kind of person who would never
admit at the office that she had gotten up at five in the morning
to watch Princess Diana's funeral even though the evening news
team was covering it and her reporter only had to do follow-up
in the weeks to come. But she had. She had even taped it—and
not because she wanted to critique the anchor.

"No," Clare repeated, tensely, "Daisy chain as in, you sit in the
grass and the sun is shining and you pinch off daisies and thread
the stem of one through the stem of the next until they make a
necklace."

"Sorry."

"It's just that sometimes you shouldn't jag on everything."

"Sorry, Clare. I am. I mean it. Go on."

"I know it sounds bizarre. Maybe epiphanies are by definition
bizarre—striking out of something ordinary. It's just that I suddenly realized that life was like a daisy chain, all of these fragile
links, little details that determine the grand scheme. It's not a
Wedding or a Job or Cancer. It's the fact that my boss had heartburn from eating osso bucco one day and took it out on me by
sending me downtown without supper to cover my least favorite
kind of art and there was this guy in black glasses with dimples
who knew where to order good vegetable samosas. And that was

Michael. So see, my whole life turned on somebody else's heartburn."

JoJo laughed. She remembered that boss.

Clare said, "So this tape was like one daisy in the chain. If I hadn't come across it, everything would've turned out differently. Everything."

As the tape pulled up short, Clare's eyes searched the road ahead for the next place to pull over. She thought she remembered a Mobil station, and as she came around a long bend, she saw the sign above the trees. She signaled for the exit and took the ramp too fast. Her tires screeched.

Pulling into the station, she darted across the pavement and angled the car in by the dumpster. She punched in the number of Michael's car phone. He answered.

"Could I just say something?" she asked him.

"Sure."

"I really do love you."

"I know you do, Clare."

"And I'm sorry."

"I am too," he said.

"Will you meet me in Mystic, at the lobster place? I won't keep you long."

—⟶⟵—

Clare figured he couldn't have left the house sooner than an hour after she did. He had still been wet from his shower, wrapped in a towel when Del called. He had been trying to pull on his pants when Clare was throwing her duffel bag in the car. She had never unpacked it from her trip to Maine. What did that mean?

Parked in the Lobster-in-the-Rough's gravel lot, she fiddled with the radio, expecting a long wait. But Michael had a heavier foot on the gas pedal than she did. His fuzz-buster had saved him more than once, and once it hadn't. He still hated the state of Florida for that speeding ticket. Clare thought of it when she saw him pull into the parking lot. His driving had always been the most aggressive thing about him. He was only ten minutes behind her.

It was an odd time of day for lobster, still morning, so their cars were the only vehicles in the wide part of the lot. A few employees in red-striped aprons set napkins out on the picnic tables, but otherwise there were few people around. Later, the place would be thick with tourists. And anyway, they weren't here to eat.

Clare walked into her husband's arms and tightened hers around him. "Don't ever let me go," she whispered.

"I wouldn't," he said. "I wouldn't, Clare."

He took her hand, and they walked past the order windows and past all the picnic tables and down to the end of the pier, where they sat on the edge and dangled their feet. The sun was a rippling glare on the water, hard in their eyes. Hers hurt, welled with tears. But then she was on the verge anyway.

"I don't mean to abandon you," he said. He looked at their hands, lying together in her lap.

"I know."

"But, Clare . . . I don't want to be cruel. And this isn't about getting even . . . but you abandoned me first."

She looked at him.

His eyes were steady in hers, filled with his characteristic calmness. He said, "Think how I felt. My wife had cancer, followed by this traumatic surgery and radiation therapy. And the next thing I know, she's flying away to Los Angeles."

"I needed the distraction," she said weakly.

"My head could reason that out. But we're not talking about our heads, are we?"

She grinned out of one side of her mouth, shook her head. No. This wasn't about their heads.

He went on: "And what was going on in River Port was consuming anyway. There was so much they needed, that I just kept giving. And now if I let up at all, I just feel as though I'm abandoning them. I've let them get so dependent on me."

She nodded.

"I've always, all my life, thought I had to protect them," he said. "Everybody was always staring at them, saying things like, *Better adjust my glasses, I'm seeing double.* And they were just so feckless. They lived in their own little world, and they had no idea about living in the real one. I used to read the maps when we went on vacation. They just thought they'd mosey into the right place, just magically. They thought the rules applied to everybody but them."

"Their little elf," she said, squeezing his hand.

"And I can't just turn that off," he said. "Intellectually I know it's not true, but I feel like I'm the only one who can protect them—from themselves and from everybody else."

"Are you?" she asked softly. "Are you protecting them?" She looked at him. It wasn't her intent to be cruel, and she wanted him to see.

He sighed, met her eye. He shook his head.

They sat there in silence, holding hands.

Finally, he shuddered as if to shake off his thoughts. He asked, "Where were you going today?"

"Back to Maine," she admitted. She told him about Riley and the accident. She told him what had almost happened.

"Do you love him?" Michael asked when she had finished. There was a tautness in his manner she had almost never seen.

Clare stared out at the boats, at the way they moved through the water, cutting it so that it folded behind them, creased with the sun, golden. "I do love him," she said.

His body hardened. He tried to pull away.

She said, "Michael, listen, I love him the way I love that seventeen-year-old who was me. I love him like I love that summer, those days on the island. I love him like yesterday."

"But you still love me?"

"Oh, Michael," she said, drawing him close. "I love you like tomorrow. Like forever."

In waning sunlight, Clare drove far down the peninsula and then turned down Folsom's road, going by the Yorks with the satellite dish, then up the hill twice, and finally down the spur by the mired tractor. She was headed for the house shadowed by the great lobster boat called *Eclipse.*

She had told Michael, as they sat on the pier facing that Connecticut inlet, that she felt she had to go back to Riley, had to do what she could. Just as he felt he had to go back to River Port.

As Clare pulled into the driveway, the two little girls came to stand at the screen door. "Mumma," Clare heard Mandy yell, "Clare Mac is back." It sounded as though she were tattling.

Laurie came out as though to stand between Clare and the children.

"Can we talk?" Clare asked.

"You've done enough damage," Laurie said. "Don't you think?"

"I want you to understand."

"I understand just fine."

"No, you don't." Clare nodded at the kids. "Can we walk?"

Laurie didn't answer. She just led Clare down toward the orchard, winding between the hulking boat and the house. It was the way they had gone before. "Mum," the little one called.

"Stay there, Jessie," Laurie barked.

When they were hidden in the trees, Clare said, "I had cancer last year." She thought it was the first time she had ever declared it out loud to anyone, and here it was in the least likely circumstances. "I had a double mastectomy, to try to prevent any more from happening. Because my mother died of it, and I have a lousy gene."

"I'm sorry," Laurie said, though she didn't sound it. "Is that why you're telling me—so I'll say, 'Oh, you've suffered so much. Here, take my husband?' "

Clare winced. "I don't want your husband," she said. "I love Riley. I do love him. But not in the way you think. I have a husband I love that way. I love him very much."

"Then what do you want with my husband?"

"I want what you wanted from me. I want to help."

"By sleeping with him?" Laurie's tone cut the air between them like a machete, quick and lethal.

"It only looked that way, Laurie," she said. "I promise you. I didn't betray my husband. And Riley didn't betray you."

"You think I'm stupid because I've lived in Sky Hill all my life and done a man's laundry and diapered his kids while you were off doing your television shows and living in some skyscraper. You think you can sidle in here and teach me a thing or two about my own husband."

"No," Clare said. "I think that because of what I've learned about myself . . . maybe because of the cancer. Because of whatever, I think I can show Riley something about himself. And I'm just asking you to let me try. Will you, Laurie?"

⌒

Laurie met Clare at the landing in time for the last ferry. She was holding Mandy's hand. "You're gonna ride over to Ledgemere with Clare Mac," she told the little girl. "And you'll get to see Daddy and stay with Aunt Kim, just like I promised."

"And build a fairy house?" Mandy demanded.

Laurie hesitated.

"Sure," Clare said. She held out her hand to the girl. But Mandy kept ahold of her mother until Captain Barnicle lifted her giggling onto his shoulders and took her aboard the *Nora B.*

Laurie let Clare get almost to the top of the gangway; then she called out to her.

Clare turned, took a few steps back toward Riley's wife.

Laurie looked down, then up. "Thank you," she said. "Thank you for trying." She bit her lip, held it still.

"Don't . . ." Clare said, waving an absolving hand. She smiled and turned back toward the boat and boarded it.

Laurie stood on the landing and waved them out of sight. Even then, when her mother was not even a visible speck, Mandy stood facing back toward Sky Hill, ignoring Clare. After a while, Clare said, "You can see the island out there."

"So?"

"I bet you'll be able to see your daddy's hair before you can see anything else about the place."

Mandy glanced over her shoulder quickly, as though Clare wouldn't be able to tell she was interested if she was swift enough about it. "He doesn't know I belong to him anymore," Mandy said, merely stating a fact.

"Oh, I think he knows that you belong to him," Clare told her. "It's just that he's forgotten how that happens. I mean how that happens every day. He's forgotten how to belong to *you*. And that makes him embarrassed."

Mandy bunched up her face, confused.

"I bet there were things you remember that your daddy used to do for you, just little things every day. Aren't there?"

"Chocolate milk," Mandy confirmed. "When Mum wasn't looking, he'd pour chocolate milk on my Froot Loops. Instead of white like you're supposed to."

"Sure," Clare laughed. "That's exactly what I mean."

"And he used to eat Bugles off his fingers, and when Jessie would cry in the car because Mummy was slow in the store, he'd put raspberries on her toes and tell her to eat 'em. And she would, she'd eat 'em off her toes. Gross!" Mandy doubled over in her glee.

"Pretty gross," Clare agreed.

Mandy was wound up now. "And he always told us to toot in the bathtub because it would make bubbles and be like having our own hot tub, like the summer complaints do, and once Jessie was trying so hard to toot that she squeezed out a poop." She said this last word in a hushed voice, then dramatically clamped a hand over her mouth.

Clare laughed and saw some of the summer people slide their eyes over and smirk to each other. She met their eyes, smiled at them, tried to disarm them with candor.

"That was really really really gross," Mandy exclaimed. " 'Cause I was in there with her, and I was the one who got spanked 'cause I tried to get away from the poop, and Mum said I coulda got hurt climbing the wall like that. And Jessie just sat there grinning, and Daddy was laughing so much he had tears coming out. Silly little Daddy!"

"Wow," Clare said. "You remember a lot."

"You don't just forget your daddy," Mandy said, suddenly solemn.

⌒⌒⌒

From the ferry, Clare and Mandy couldn't spot Riley at the landing. "Where is his old carrot top?" Mandy fretted, more to herself than to anyone else.

"Don't worry," Captain Barnicle told her, "he'll be lurking about somewhere." Then he looked meaningfully at Clare.

"Still?" she asked.

"Tries to disguise it, though," the captain answered.

True enough, Riley came out of the nearest fish house the minute he saw Clare. He was swathed in an apron and sloshing in his boots. "Clare Mac," he called. His face blazed.

"Daddy!" Mandy cried from the top of the captain's shoulders. She waved wildly, then added, heartbreakingly, "It's me, Mandy Bo Bandy."

Riley's eyes darted to Clare, and she reached up to take Mandy's hand. "Jump down, Mandy," she said.

The child landed and started leaping toward her father in one motion. She wrapped her arms around his legs and squeezed so hard that she grunted in the effort.

Riley smiled and laid his hand on the top of her head. But he looked like someone who had a stranger's dog sniffing amorously at his leg. He was wildly uncomfortable.

Clare said, "Mandy and I thought we'd come for a visit."

"Okay," he said.

Mandy took his hand and swung it. "You smell like fish," she told him.

"Yep," he said. "I was helping old Smirky Jones with his bait. It stinks, doesn't it?"

"Peeeuwee," she affirmed.

Clare laughed, and Riley joined in, and Mandy pulled them up short by saying, "Daddy, do you remember the raspberries on Jessie's toes?"

Uncertainty pulled his brows together. He looked up at Clare from the hood of his confusion.

Mandy said, "And the poop in the tub?"

He clawed at Clare with his eyes, wanting rescue.

His daughter said, "Remember, you told her to toot, only she couldn't, and then it was gross, and you laughed so much that tears came out."

"I did, huh?" he managed.

"You don't remember," she said, disappointed. She turned to Clare in accusation, "See, he doesn't remember."

The shadows were lengthening. Their part of the world was about to tip into darkness. And Clare felt how precarious they were, riding in space, trying to help one another, trying to matter. Riley's jaw was set against her.

She walked behind him. He held Mandy's hand loosely in his, and even Mandy was stiff, taking careful steps in her little rubber-toed sneakers, watching each step in the dirt of the road. Clare recognized relief in the way Mandy dropped Riley's hand and ran toward Kim. She hugged her aunt around the neck.

Kim said, "You get to sleep in the loft with Nicky. How 'bout that?"

"Nicky!" Mandy cried, summoning her cousin, and they could

barely get the girl's attention again to tell her sleep tight and don't let the bedbugs bite. Tomorrow, Clare promised, they would do the fairy house. But Mandy was already six steps gone, and Kim stood grim-faced the whole time, her arms folded tight across her middle.

Riley was furious at Clare, at the world maybe. Without a word to her or to Kim, he stalked off. It was only because she felt obligated that Clare followed. As the sun went down, she trailed him all the way out to the shipwreck beach. She followed him all the way to the dangerous lip of it. She had never dared go that far out before. The ocean crashed at their feet. She felt the spray on her eyelids.

Riley stood with his fists knotted, then suddenly whirled on her: "What are you trying to do to me?"

"Help you," she said. Something in her was pleading for his forgiveness. Something in her feared she had gone too far, feared she had read too much into her own epiphanies.

"By breaking my heart?" he asked.

She reached for his hand. He backed off. "First you just run out on me, and then when you show up again, you've got her in tow. What is it with you? You want to hurt her too, make sure everyone suffers?"

"Maybe you're right," she said. "And maybe you're not." She stepped closer to him: "Riley, you have to start somewhere, or the suffering is not going to stop. For anybody. You have to start making some new memories, putting them up like a barrier between you and what your mind has lost."

"I am what I've lost." He hurled it at her.

"No," she said. "You're not."

His hands were knotted into fists.

"Come here," she said. She sat on a rock. "I want to tell you something."

"I don't want to hear it."

"You might."

He stood in defiance, looking at the pounding surf and the last high pink in the clouds, that last light. A wave crashed with a smacking crescendo, and she thought of the children swept off these rocks. Her impulse was to turn toward higher ground. But she ignored it. She had a purpose.

Misgivings threatened her. But she had come for one thing: to tell him about her one possible bit of wisdom and the way she had earned it. She said, "Riley, I had cancer."

He didn't move.

"I thought I was going to die like my mother, you remember? They said it would likely be all right. We caught it early. The diagnostic technology is so much better now. But I wanted to be sure. I had them take off both breasts. I insisted on it against their best arguments to the contrary, all their statistics. It was radical, they said. But I wanted radical. I was radical: I ate shark cartilage. I ate seaweed for breakfast, lunch, and dinner.

"Then one day I realized that I wasn't ever going to be sure. At any moment, whether I was standing in front of the camera at work or swimming laps in some pool or making love to Michael, at any moment, it could be slipping into my blood and traveling to my spine or to my brain or to my lungs. It could be killing me already."

He turned and looked at her a long minute. Then he came and sat next to her, took her hand between both of his.

"And when I realized that I was never going to know one hundred percent, I gave up. I became the cancer. It became the central fact of my life. It became me. It made every decision for me: no children; I might die and orphan them. No time off work; I might be so still that I could feel it working away inside me. No joy because it might not last."

The surf rose in a spray of white. It glowed in the growing dusk, close to them. It gave out a gasp, and Clare felt drops of water spatter across her face.

"We should maybe go up higher," Riley said, his muscles twitching in readiness to leave. "We'll go sit on the cliff. You'll tell me there."

"No, let's stay," she said, knowing it was a risk. "Let's live a little."

He chuckled at the irony of her saying that. "And you expect me not to love you?" he asked.

"I was coming back to you," she said. "You should know that. You should know what you've meant to me. That I haven't been playing with you. I was coming back."

His eyes swung to hers, latched, seemed to grope through the coming night to get at her meaning, to get farther into it.

She told him: "I had decided that I was full of this pain, and you were full of yours, and that maybe our misery made us right for each other. Maybe everything that had gone wrong for each of us made us right for one another. Maybe there was enough wrong to make it right that I should walk away from my marriage and you should walk away from yours and from your kids.

"But I was in my car, driving up here, and I heard this tape. I had made it by accident, and it had caught a conversation between Michael and me, years ago when we were first married. When we were happy. And it reminded me that our happiness wasn't made of grand things that people write operas about. It was about certain comfort. About coming home from work, sloshing through the snow from the subway, and seeing a light on in the apartment and knowing he's already there. He's waiting. It's about going to the farmers' market on Saturday and baking bread on a rainy night and eating supper in your stocking feet. It was about sitting on the same couch.

"And, cancer or no cancer, I can sit on the same couch with

my husband. I can be happy in the only way happiness exists: snatches of moments, fleeting seconds. Just like making a daisy chain. You remember those daisy chains?"

He nodded, and after a pause asked, "So where does that leave me, Clare?" There was agitation ragged in his voice. "It's all gone, except what I had with you. Everything's black. I don't remember coming home to any lights in any windows. I don't remember."

"Get out of your own way," she said.

"What's that supposed to mean?" He bristled.

"Do you want a life with Laurie and the kids?"

His frustration crackled off him. It was as though he were a taut wire, mute itself but with the wind vibrating through it, moaning. "Don't be cruel," he said. "I want whatever I can have. I want to be happy. I want to remember what made me happy."

"I think you can," she said.

"The doctors said the longer I go without..."

"Forget the doctors. Forget the diagnosis. Forget what's already happened, okay?"

He looked at her as though even in the darkness he would be able to see how she had let herself slip past reality, as though he could see the sheen of her madness, this madness.

"Do you know how an eclipse works?" she asked him.

"Not again, Clare Mac..."

"No, listen. It's the way I explained my problem to myself." She lined up three pebbles on his knee. "Sun, earth, moon," she said.

"Sun, earth, moon," he repeated, though his frustration fuzzed like static around every word.

"Okay, you remember our eclipse?"

"Ours," he echoed bitterly.

"The moon was full and bright because the sun was shining on it from the other side of the world, right? And then the black crept across it."

He nodded.

"That was the shadow of the earth. The earth got in the way."

"I know that," he said.

"Okay, so you're the earth," she said. "The blackness you see now is your own shadow."

He breathed out confusion, impatience.

She said, "No, listen. You look at Mandy, and all you see is that you don't remember. She's got this shadow across her. It obscures her, and you can't see that she's an adorable little girl and that you can fall in love with her all over again."

He sighed and thumped his head so hard it made a cracking noise. "I have an injury to my brain, Clare. That's the goddamn shadow."

"Riley," she said. "Forget that, okay? I can't do anything about that. You can't do anything about it. The doctors can't. But the sun is still shining. You're still alive, and if you look at Mandy and see only blackness, you're seeing your own shadow. You're getting in your own way, eclipsing that little kid."

"I didn't do this to myself, Clare. It happened to me."

"That's true. Past tense. Now you have a choice. You can get out of your own way and see where the sunshine lands. You can stop eclipsing every moment that might make you happy."

They sat there, and the sea moved higher on the rocks, threw itself farther toward them every time. But they stayed, and when the full moon rose out of the sea, Clare saw it even though she was looking not at it but at Riley. She said, "I just saw the moon rise in your eyes."

New York had already gone into the early dusk of its tall buildings.
The last of the sunlight had climbed to the top of the tallest buildings, then, and finally jumped off the top. It was true twilight now.
The sky was that soft luminous blue going black, and the windows
stood out like stars. Clare and JoJo had walked to the West Side and
were sitting side by side in the plaza at Lincoln Center.

Clare kept her eyes on the crowd streaming into Alice Tully
Hall for the evening's Mozart. She was tired from talking all afternoon, but relieved too. When they were roommates, she and
JoJo used to say that no event in either of their lives was real until
they told the other one every detail. It was still true. Sometimes

even as it was happening, Clare was thinking how she would put it to Jo. She was already telling it as a story.

Now she wound this one up. She said, "Do you see what I mean about it being like a daisy chain? From the postcard to the tape, nothing but a string of fragile little things."

JoJo sighed. She had one hand dangling in the fountain.

Clare told her, "If I didn't know better, Jo, I'd think you were a little choked up."

"Nah," JoJo said, her voice cracking. "But it's just so sad. I think we'd better go to Serendipity for frozen hot chocolate."

"It's not so sad," Clare protested. "Not really. Not the way it came out."

"Not for you maybe. Or Michael," JoJo said. "But do you really think there's any way that poor guy can come to a happy ending?"

"Riley?" Clare asked, surprised at her friend's question.

JoJo said, "I mean I love The Michael, and of course I'm glad you worked it out. Wouldn't that have been the irony of ironies if I had finally gotten married and then you let your marriage dissolve, poof?"

"I wasn't going to let that happen."

"You almost did," JoJo said. "But anyway, I'm not talking about happy or sad for you. I know you. I know you're just as happy being a little sad. Otherwise you wouldn't ever have an excuse to eat raw cookie dough."

"Thanks for your sympathy."

"But, Riley, what does he have really? Not you. His wife is a shrew. He can't work. His kid can't stop talking about bodily emissions."

Clare laughed. "Laurie's not so bad, Jo. She's just hurt to the marrow. She loves him. And Mandy's flat-out adorable. If you could've seen her with him, you wouldn't worry about Riley. That little girl is the moon and all the stars." Clare told JoJo how Mandy had raced ahead of her and Riley that last day, how her little red head had flashed in the sunlight that splintered through the spires of fir: like a bird in flight. She disappeared behind stands of ferns. She shimmied up standing tree snags and looked into the wood-pecker holes. She crawled between moss-humped stumps. "I found another one," she would cry and come running back to them. "You have to see it. It's the cutest thing."

She had held out her hand for a penny, and Riley had given her one. She ran back up the trail.

Clare observed, "She's had a lot of practice at this."

"Obviously," Riley said.

They were out there looking for fairy houses, the tiny dwellings that children constructed out of twigs and fir cones and clumps of lichen, whatever was available along the paths of Worship Forest, where the trees were towering and gothic as a great cathedral. The pennies left by hikers were supposedly for the fairies, but it was commonly known that an old islander named Betsy, who wore a kerchief on her head and carried a basket, came down the path every Tuesday to clear encroaching poison ivy. And she took the pennies. Which in no way ruined the fairy-tale quality, because, moving among the shafts of light in the forest, Betsy looked very much like something out of Grimm's.

"See," Mandy cried to them, as Clare and Riley rounded a curve and saw her crouching near a crevice in some rocks. "That's the bed, and that's the table, and these are the bushes by the door." She pointed at tufts of moss and pinecones that revealed more about Mandy's imagination than about the last child's intentions.

Riley's daughter bounced back to her feet, brushed the fir nee-dles off her knees, and said, "We've got to find the perfect place, the perfect place, the perfect place." She chanted to herself as she scouted ahead of them. Her plan was that the three of them would build a village of fairy houses.

Riley said quietly to Clare, "You're really leaving tomorrow?"

She nodded. "Michael's meeting me in Camden. We're going to Acadia to cycle on the carriage paths."

"He's the luckiest man alive," Riley said.

"One of them." She hooked her pinkie in his littlest finger, held on for a few steps while Mandy was out of sight. "I'll miss you."

"No, you won't."

"Of course I will, Riley. You've given me things no one else ever has. No one ever could."

"A concussion?"

"That too." She laughed, then ticked off a list. "The eclipse, for one. And I never would have jumped off into Jade without you."

From up ahead, Mandy crowed.

"My daughter, the rooster," Riley said.

Mandy appeared on the path, hopping from one foot to another. Both her arms were flung in the air. "I found our place. I found it. I found it."

Her proposed site was nestled in a grove of seedlings. The tiny fir trees sprung from a mossy floor that looked every bit the village green. "You go there, Clare Mac," the child instructed, "and this is my place. And Daddy, you get the hilltop." The hilltop was a disintegrating stump. There were mushrooms growing on it.

Clare set to work snapping twigs as logs for a cabin, and plucking fir cones into pieces, each one a little shingle. She laid tiny stones as a path and decorated the interior with a red toadstool and a lacy bit of lichen.

As absorbed as she was in the task, Clare still managed to keep an eye on Riley and Mandy. The little girl hummed as she worked and punctuated her progress with chortles of exuberance. And Riley, though he was busy framing up a tepee, was more caught up in watching Mandy and slipping her his special discoveries— a feather, a toadstool with red dots, a curl of birch bark to use as smoke from her rolled-leaf chimney. "Put it just like that," he told her, balancing on his haunches to attach it to the chimney.

Mandy clasped her hands at her throat, and in admiration exclaimed, "Oh, Daddy, you always make it the best. It looks just like smoke!" And then she threw her arms around his neck.

He lost his balance and fell back on the thick cushion of evergreen needles, back into a shaft of sunlight that had pierced the treetop canopy. And Mandy didn't let go. She toppled too and kept him in her embrace and hovered over his face, kissing the tip of his nose and the bit of skin between his eyebrows. "Silly little Daddy," she murmured. Then, slowly, sweetly, she kissed him right in the middle of his smile.

_ᴄ᷂3ᴄ᷂2_

Clare looked at JoJo in the fine silver light of the great plaza. She asked her, "How many years have we been friends?"

JoJo shrugged, "Twelve, maybe."

Clare shook her head. "Twelve years, and that's the first tear I've seen you shed."

"Didn't someone say something about frozen hot chocolate?" JoJo muttered, getting up and slinging her weighty purse over her shoulder. She bounced a little on the balls of her feet, like a runner warming up for a circuit of the park reservoir.

Clare stood and hooked an arm through her friend's elbow. "I love you, Jo," she said.

JoJo snorted. Her eyelashes were still glistening.

"I do," Clare said.

"I love you too," JoJo said. "But could you cut me a little slack? I'm supposed to be the one with the crazy up-and-down life. I can't take this from you."

"Okay."

"Promise?" JoJo asked.

"Promise," Clare told her, and as she followed JoJo to the near-est crosstown bus stop, she thought it was a vow she could keep.

The days she and Michael had spent in Acadia had been re-storative. By the time she drove farther up the coast to meet her husband, Clare had finished her good-byes to Riley and his family. And Michael, when he got to the hotel—only two hours late— said he had persuaded Del to accept the help available through the Alzheimer's Association. That morning, she had been sitting with a social worker, interviewing in-home health-care workers. "Oh, Michael," Clare had said, because what else was there? And they had stood in one another's embrace for a long time.

They had reservations in an old hotel that had once been grand. It was built of rock with a deep shady porch. The lobby had a fireplace and beautiful worn Persian rugs, and there was only the one hand-crank elevator big enough for a single person and the luggage. Upstairs, the hallways were narrow, but their room opened out onto a balcony overlooking a bay. The first morning they were there, Clare had woken early and lain warm against Michael and had watched the sun come up out of the Atlantic. She watched the colors come back into the world and thought how they were coming back into hers.

She and Michael talked some about what they had been through—together, separately. But mostly they climbed back into a shared sense of life. They hiked one sunrise to the top of Cadillac Mountain, which made everything seem small, towering as it did above the ocean and the tiny offshore islands. On other afternoons, they ate steaming popovers overlooking Jordan Pond and its sheer depths. And every day, they biked for hours and hours along the carriage paths that smelled of balsam and salt air. Clare loved the long downhills where the wind rushed over her face, through her hair. She loved flying in and out of the shadows of the great trees, light and dark, light and dark, light and dark.

One day, when they stopped on a high ledge to split an apple, Michael's skin smelled of that wind. She couldn't stop breathing him in. They were sitting together on a mossy rock that gave them a view of the mountains around them, a steep valley below. They were comfortably quiet for many minutes, and then Michael spoke. "What do you think of the name Emma for a girl?" he asked tentatively.

The question ran through Clare like the first touch of a new lover. She smiled, though it almost broke into tears. "It's nice," she said. Then, though her lips twitched around the words, she added, "I've been thinking about the name Daisy. Do you think it's too frilly—or maybe too outlandish?"

Michael didn't try to hide the tears that flooded into his eyes. "It's beautiful, Clare," he said, gathering her closer to him and letting go a breath he seemed to have been holding for too long. "It's the most beautiful thing I've ever heard."